failing minds.

a seductively sinister story about the human brain.

Keeping Minds Book 2

by Vinal Lang

Vinal Lang

As you read this book, keep in mind that some things may not make sense at first. Please just keep reading, and they will all fall into place. The story is based on fictional locations, events and characters.

Since I am expecting that you have read the first book, Keeping Minds, then you know some of what to expect as far as content, however this time it will be darker and more disturbing. We will deal with a completely different topic of the human brain and mind; mental illness. If you have not read the first book, Keeping Minds, please do so before continuing as it will make this book a much more amazing experience.

This book contains mature, adult content, even more than before.

Please read with the expectation of disturbingly shocking and twisted, unedited adult human behavior.

V.2

Copyright © 2022 Vinal Lang

ISBN: 1659042689
ISBN-13: 978-1659042689

Vinal Lang

This is the second book in the *Keeping Minds* series. **If you have not read the novel *Keeping Minds* then please do so first.**

The timeline of this story does *not* pick up where the first book left off. Instead, it roughly follows the same timeline as the first book.

This is the darker story of some other characters and how their lives are intertwined with the characters from *Keeping Minds*, as the two stories run parallel to each other. You will see how characters that you never saw, affected the events of the first book.

The days of the week are not frequently mentioned as I do not want you to focus on petty details. There are, however, events that you will easily recognize, and this will allow you to thoughtlessly follow the timeline as you become fully immersed in the story.

As you read this book, please remember that some things may not make sense at first. Please just keep reading, and it will all fall into place.

the chapters.

****

*"There is nothing either good or bad, but thinking
makes it so."*

-Shakespeare

****

Vinal Lang

Chapter 1 – A Perfect Couple.

Jill woke up in her bed. The morning sun illuminated the room with a beautiful orange glow. She stretched, yawned, and then rolled over onto her side.

She watched light specs of dust floating in the golden beams of the late morning sun. The backdrop was a view from a medium-sized window of the tall, brick, thirty-five-story building across the street.

James was lying in bed next to her, still asleep. She lay still and looked at him, his shirtless body, his tattoos. She loved everything about this man...well, almost everything.

James was her other half. The couple had been almost inseparable since they'd met again a few years ago.

Jill stared at his face, so handsome and chiseled. James' blonde hair fell across it as he slept. She reached over and brushed it away with her fingers, making his body twitch a little in response to her soft touch.

James started to stir.

"Hey. Good morning," Jill whispered softly.

"Hey," James replied quietly, keeping his eyes closed. He rolled over, turning his back to Jill. "I'm still mad at you," he said.

Jill couldn't for the life of her remember what they had fought about. She couldn't recall why James would even have a reason to be mad at her.

She slowly stood up with a soft sigh. Her cat, Kitty, ran up to greet her. Purring loudly, he brushed softly against her legs, making her smile like he always did.

Jill looked at herself in the bedroom mirror. "I look like I need more sleep," she said quietly, as she rubbed her face.

She was a tall, curvy, gorgeous brunette. Her hair was wavy, dark brown, and fell to about the middle of her back. Her body was perfect. Jill slightly resembled a tattooed, 1950s pinup model. She was nearly every man's vintage fantasy.

Jill was very sexy but also very rough around the edges—vulgar and sassy, yet quiet and refined. She had learned to be whatever she needed to be for whatever situation in which she found herself.

It was about ten in the morning. Jill didn't have to be at work, serving drinks at a local bar, until later that night.

She walked into the bathroom to start getting ready for the day. On the counter, she saw a dusty, white plastic bag. It was empty, other than a little bit of leftover white powder. Cocaine.

Jill nonchalantly threw the bag in the garbage can and looked at herself more closely in the mirror. She had red marks at the bottom of her neck and small bruises on her arms.

She yawned, stretched, and then brushed her teeth. She wasn't going to let James' bad attitude ruin her entire day.

The couple shared a small one-bedroom apartment in the city. It was comfortable and cozy, made that way mostly by Jill

She looked around, overwhelmed at the sight of the mess and clutter, made that way mostly by James.

Jill sighed.

She had some errands to run, and it would be good to get away for a while anyway. She could deal with the mess later. Instead, she grabbed her laundry basket full of dirty clothes and walked down to the laundromat just a few blocks away.

She put the couple's clothes into the large machine and then fed it soap and quarters. The washer started to foam and slosh. Jill watched through the glass door. That's how her life felt right now. *When is* my *spin cycle ever going to end?* she thought.

Jill set a timer on her phone. Forty five minutes. She left her laundry and the empty basket and walked down to one of the city's libraries. She sat and read everything from the current news to erotic, romance, smut novels.

Reading let her escape her world. It let her escape her life—not that things were horrible, but they definitely could have been better.

James seemed to be getting more angry and violent lately. He had also become more controlling. Jill was getting into fights with him more often. She just wished he weren't so irate and short-tempered. James was the man she loved, and the way he was acting broke her heart.

Jill finished the last page of the fashion magazine she was reading, just in time for her phone alarm to go off. Her laundry needed to be switched over.

Jill walked back into the laundromat, took her damp clothes out of the giant washing machine, and put them in an equally big industrial drier. She fed the machine quarters and set her timer once again.

She walked back to the library and started on a new book that had caught her eye — *Sustainable Artist*. Jill sat down in the quiet library and began to read.

Back home, James mumbled "Ugh..." as he rolled out of bed and into the bathroom.

He looked at himself in the mirror; his bright, crystal-blue eyes stared vacantly back at him. He had small bruises on his arms and chest and a very large bruise, about the size of a softball, was on his right thigh. "Fuck..." he said, running his fingers through his golden-blonde hair.

James and Jill were a rough couple. Jill generally didn't back down from James, and this caused quite a few physical fights — usually one every couple of months.

James threw a shirt on and got back in their small, unmade double bed.

He was currently unemployed, but sometimes he picked up the odd job that came along.

James lay in bed and thought about how he wanted to get high. Drugs let him escape his world. They let him escape his life. He wanted to forget everything, but he didn't have any drugs left.

James had finished what had been left in the bag of coke last night while Jill had been asleep, and they definitely didn't have any money to buy more.

He lay in their small, messy one-bedroom apartment in the dirty part of the city and thought about their last fight and how he probably overreacted. This reality was quickly brushed aside as James wasn't one to back down either. He would never admit that anything was wrong. He would never admit that he needed help.

James read the new messages on his prepaid cell phone, replying to the important ones, and then he smiled, closed his eyes, and lay his head back down on the pillow.

Back in the silence of the library, the alarm on Jill's phone went off, quietly notifying her with a vibration.

Her clothes were done, and it was time to head back to the laundromat. As she sat and folded their worn-out clothes, she thought about everything that was happening in her life. Something needed to change for them.

She put the folded clothes in the basket and slowly walked home, taking her time to admire everything along the way. The way the air smelled like smoky, grilled barbeque and the vibrant colors of the misunderstood graffiti art on the bricks that she passed. She wanted to stay away as long as possible. She didn't want any confrontation with James. The less they saw of each other right now, the better.

Jill was normally laid-back, but when challenged by James, she usually fought back, and that never ended well. Jill was tired of it all and didn't want to fight anymore.

She cautiously walked into their small apartment and set the basket of clean, folded clothes down next to a pile of clean, unfolded clothes from earlier in the week. She was fearful about which James was lying in wait for her. Most of her life was spent feeling like she was walking on eggshells.

"Hey!" James called from the bedroom.

"Hey!" Jill said, slowly walking to the bedroom door and peeking around the corner.

"Sorry about the fight. It was stupid!" James said with little emotion. He was still in bed.

An apology was unusual for James, especially right now.

"Thank you. I love you! I don't ever want you to be mad at me, you know that," Jill said, as she climbed back into bed with her lover. She quickly fell asleep next to the man she admired with every fiber of her being.

The perfect couple peacefully slept intertwined.

Chapter 2 – Freaking Out.

Jill awoke, only a few hours later, to the sound of James rummaging through drawers in the bathroom.

"What are you doing?" she called out sleepily.

"I'm looking for something to take; I'm freaking out...my head. I need something to take the edge off," James mumbled loudly, as he knocked things off the counter and onto the bathroom floor.

"We don't have anything," Jill said with a wince, knowing that her answer was not going to go over well.

"Fuuuuuck!" James yelled.

Jill covered her ears. His voice made her want to crawl away to a secret place and hide. She felt like there was nothing she could do to comfort him when he was like this. She felt helpless.

"I'm going to work tonight. I'll make some money to get you something," Jill reassured him.

She got out of bed and cautiously got her purse from the counter. She dug through it for a minute, finally finding what she was looking for. The two white pills that she remembered losing a while ago were now sticky and covered with fuzz and lint.

She cautiously approached the bathroom; the sound of anger grew louder, as James was now trembling and knocking things over.

"Here, I found these at the bottom of my pur—"

Before Jill could finish, James had snatched the fuzzy pills from her hand and washed them down with a handful of water from the bathroom sink.

"What were they?" he asked, his face flush and sweaty.

"Oxy, I think. You're lucky I found them. Why don't you go relax?"

James walked to the bed and fell down face-first.

"Oh my God! I was freaking out! Thanks, baby!" he said with a smile. "You saved me."

"I love you, babe," Jill said, sitting down next to James on the bed. She rubbed his back.

"I feel sooooo much better!" he said, as he returned to a calm, mellow state.

Sometimes Jill thought she could give James anything and he would calm down. The drugs affected him so quickly, it almost seemed like just the act of taking them had a placebo effect, calming him down before they even realistically had time to start working. Jill thought maybe it was all just in his sick mind.

"Hey, I almost forgot to tell you…I got a random text from someone that I don't know today. I think we should look into what he has to say. I don't really have any details yet; he's going to send more info tomorrow," James said, already starting to sound sleepy.

"Oh...okay. What's it about?" Jill asked, puzzled by the vague topic.

James didn't answer; he had already fallen asleep, sent off to his dreams by two mysterious, fuzzy pills.

She knew James like the back of her hand. She knew that he probably already had the details and wasn't telling her. Now, she wanted to know what he was talking about, and curiosity would get the better of her. Jill knew it was probably about some new drug connection, but she still hoped, against all odds, that it was about a new way to get the prescriptions he needed.

Jill carefully took James' phone and unlocked it. If he found out that she even knew his password, it wouldn't be pretty. She knew that she was taking a big chance. Risky.

Jill saw a text message with a list of a few names on it. One name looked familiar. "Huh?" she said quietly, as she copied the information from the text message onto a small scrap of paper. "I remember you."

She tucked the paper into her bra.

Jill quietly put the phone back and left James sleeping alone in the apartment. She headed back down to the library to do some research.

The afternoon sun was warm and cheery. The city was cooled by a nice, soft breeze.

She did a little bit of her own investigating, looking up the information, written on the scrap of paper, that she had hidden in her bra.

The information gave her an idea—a way to get the prescription drugs that James desperately needed.

It looked like she would be going to a party tomorrow night, instead of trying to pick up an extra shift at the bar. She wrote the information down on a sticky note; a name and address. She folded the note up and tucked in her bra with the other scrap of paper.

But for tonight, unfortunately, she still had to work.

Jill read for several hours, becoming absorbed by the stories. The words pulled her in and made her forget her reality. This was her world now; she could be Alice in Wonderland, she could be anything she read and imagined.

The day passed quickly, and it was now almost time to get ready for work, so Jill headed home.

She got home with little time to do anything other than change her clothes. James was nowhere to be found.

Jill was back out the front door and headed down the street in under fifteen minutes. Almost a new record.

Chapter 3 – A Woman Everybody Wants.

Jill was sitting on the crowded train as it rolled along the rickety tracks, taking her to work.

The cars rattled and shook as the wheels clinked on the rails. Jill was pretty sure that she was riding the same exact train that she rode with her mom as a little girl. It smelled old and seemed to be falling apart—loose, rusty bolts and torn, tattered seats.

Jill stared out the scratched, dirty window, thinking about her life with James. She knew that something had to change soon. She thought about how much she loved that man. She just wanted to have a normal, stable life like other couples.

The train approached Jill's stop with a rumble, snapping her out of her daydream of a perfect life with her lover. She kept smiling, even as the thought faded away.

As Jill stepped off the train, the reality of her life hit her hard. She walked about a half a block past the dirty buildings of bricks and graffiti, stopping at the door to the hole-in-the-wall bar where she worked. A downtown pub.

Jill walked into the dark, mostly empty bar. The place was a mess because nobody fucking cared, except her.

She started cleaning up after the bartender who had been scheduled before her.

She cut limes and lemons, filled the cooler, and wiped everything down.

Jill hated her job.

"So, how are you doing tonight?" Jill chatted with a regular patron.

"I'm good! It was a rough day at work, but all in all it wasn't too bad," the man said.

"That's good," Jill replied, wishing she could say the same for herself.

"Did you go to that concert over the weekend?" Jill asked. She didn't really care at all, but she knew that the idle chitchat with men at the bar was what brought money in.

Jill half-listened, nodded, and agreed on cue as if she was genuinely interested. She was good at pretending, because she had been doing it for so many years.

Jill had spent a lot of time pretending to be something she wasn't. She felt like she had to be a more socially acceptable version of herself or people were quick to look down on her.

James was the only person who she felt really knew who she was. Everyone else seemed so superficial and judgmental while at the same time being completely fake themselves.

"I'm so glad that your son got into the college he wanted. That's good to hear," Jill responded with false interest to another man later in the evening.

"That's interesting. You will have to tell me more about that later," she said to a different middle-aged man, referring to talk of a new convertible sports car he'd just purchased. Jill was honestly hoping that he would forget later...she didn't fucking care.

This was just a small sample of multiple other fake conversations Jill had throughout the night, every one of them just a desperate attempt to make as much money as she could.

"Fuck that guy!" Jill cursed loudly, realizing that one man left without paying his tab. Now she was going to have to cover his fifty-six-dollar bill before she left tonight. Jill was frustrated.

"Can I get a smoke?" she asked a coworker.

The woman handed her a cigarette, and Jill headed out the back door to the alley behind the restaurant. At the sound of her opening the door, a couple of rats scurried from the pile of garbage next to the small set of steps.

Jill sat down on the steps alone and smoked the single cigarette. She listened somberly to the city sounds. She had learned to hate them. To her, the sounds evoked memories of everything she had been through here in this godforsaken city. For once, she wanted to just get away to someplace quiet...maybe the mountains...or the desert.

*Someday...*she thought to herself, as she puffed the thick, white smoke.

"Fifty-six dollars...Goddamn it!" she mumbled to herself, as she thought again about the money she now owed. She fought her negative thoughts away as her hazel eyes started to water. She finished up the cigarette, which hadn't really made her feel any better, and headed back into hell.

Jill dragged herself through the rest of the night, serving drinks, flirting with drunk barflies, trying to make as much money as she could. Getting enough money for James' prescription medication was the only thing on her mind the entire night.

James was severely bipolar and needed prescription medication to help him function normally. He had been off them for a couple of unbearable months now. It wouldn't be so unmanageable but he had turned to street drugs. Cocaine, heroin, oxy, meth; these drugs turned a treatable illness into an uncontrollable demon.

This was why he had become so angry and violent. Sometimes his mood would instantly change to melancholy and depressed. Recently though, it had started to become different. The bad times weren't leveling off; his anger just continued escalating. Jill was almost at the end of her rope.

Finally, 2 a.m. rolled around—last call.

"Thank God!" Jill said, happy that the long night was finally over.

She wiped the counters and mopped the floors. She closed up the bar and counted her tips.

Forty-five dollars...

An exhausted Jill double-checked her math. After the fifty-six-dollar tab she had to cover because of the asshole who didn't pay, her total was correct.

She had busted her ass all night for forty-five fucking dollars! It was just a quarter of the cost of James' prescriptions for one month and she still had to pay rent and the electricity bill.

Jill was struggling.

The exhausted, but still gorgeous, brunette bartender bummed another cigarette off the bar manager as she locked the front door for the night.

"Thanks, I have a lighter," Jill said.

They said goodnight to each other, and then they went their separate ways, leaving the locked bar behind.

Jill lit the cigarette and started walking. She had decided to walk home so she could save the three dollars in train fare.

As she walked down the dark, menacing streets, Jill weighed her options. She needed more cash. There was really only one she could come up with. It was a last-resort option that she hated even considering.

It looked like she was going to have to strip a couple of nights again this month. Jill bit her nails, and her hazel eyes started to water.

For as much as she loved James with her whole heart, sometimes she fucking hated that man almost an equal amount.

As she walked along through the dark night, she reluctantly called the manager of one of the local strip clubs. Jill knew him well. She could always get any drugs that she wanted from the burly but suave man.

Jill had been clean for over five years now, but she still bought drugs for James when she could.

"Hey, Jill! What do you need, sweety? Let me guess; you left your white shirt here?" the man on the phone said.

"No, none of that. I just need some extra money and wondered if I could come in and work for a couple of nights," Jill said, as she bit her bottom lip.

"Oh, of course. You know I love seeing you naked, and so do the clients! You bring this club big money on the nights you work. Come in any night this week," the gruff voice said.

Jill cringed at the tasteless compliment from the equally tasteless man.

"Thanks...I'll be in this week," she said with a sigh, as she surrendered the little bit of self-worth she had been able to build up since the last time she'd had to strip for James' prescriptions.

Jill hung up the phone.

This is the last fucking time, she remembered promising herself a couple of months ago before snorting a bump of coke, taking her clothes off, and getting on stage. She had known deep down inside that she would probably be back—stuck in a vicious cycle.

Jill started to sob. This wasn't the life she wanted. This was hell.

"Fuck!" she screamed, punching the brick wall of the building alongside which she was walking.

"Are you okay?" the dark figure of a dirty, homeless man asked from the shadows. Jill was slightly startled as she hadn't seen him sitting there in the alley next to a city dumpster.

"Yeah, thanks; I'll be okay," she said, wiping her hazel eyes. "Things are just hard right now."

"Tell me about it," the dirty, bearded man said. "I'm trying to get clean and out of this city after a long run of bad luck. You don't happen to have any change, do you?"

"I do, but it's not much." Jill gave the man three dollars—the money she would have spent on the ride home. She also gave him a small Styrofoam box full of some leftover food from her shift. She probably wasn't going to eat the food anyway, and she would make the donated money back stripping later in the week.

"They have a really good shelter over by Eighth and Mullen. They help a lot of people, just like you, get back on their feet. You should go talk to them."

"Thank you so much!" the unkempt man said with a smile.

"My name is Jill. It was nice meeting you…"

"Jerry…my name is Jerry."

"Well, it was nice to meet you, Jerry," she said, as she waved and headed on her way with a newfound smile on her face. She forgot about her problems for a few minutes—about rent, about stripping, about James. She felt good inside. The temporary escape into happiness had been well worth three dollars.

Jill continued her walk home, picking up the pace as it started to drizzle. It looked like it was going to start storming heavily any minute. A chilly breeze set in. Jill shivered and wrapped her sweater tightly around her body.

When she finally got home early in the morning, Jill found the apartment a mess—more so than usual, that is—and James was nowhere to be found.

"Damn it!" Jill said.

Jill looked at herself in the mirror. Her body was covered in cold, wet clothes.

Jill slowly took her clothes off. She reached back and unclasped her red lace bra, sending an instant chill across her entire body. The bra fell to the floor in a tangle of rain-soaked red lace, landing on top of her discarded work clothes. Next, she slowly slid the damp, black-and-red lace panties down her long legs.

Jill stood, exposed, looking at the naked woman in the reflection. Her brown hair was wet and messy from the rain. She looked at her sexy, seductive body—the same voluptuous body she'd had to resort to using to pay the bills on more than one occasion.

On that body, Jill always saw the bruises and scratches no matter how much they faded, no matter how much other people couldn't see them, no matter how much they physically disappeared. She still saw them.

Jill wished that, for once, she could see a plain, average woman staring back at her. She wished she saw the reflection of a boring, understated woman who had her life together. Maybe she could be a nurse someday…or even a doctor.

Jill was trying to get her life together, but James wasn't helping.

"This will be the last time," she said to the naked, seductive temptress looking back at her from the mirror, as she thought about getting naked in front of strange, horny men, for money.

Jill got her phone out and called James. He didn't answer.

She was too exhausted to worry about him now. She climbed into bed and slid her naked body under the covers.

As she lay in their small bed, trying to fall asleep, she watched the storm start blowing harder outside. She wondered where James was and what he was doing. She hoped he was okay.

As her heavy, hazel eyes intermittently closed, she looked over and saw her red bra lying on the bedroom floor. Inside the bright-red lace, she could see the sticky note and scrap of paper with the information from James' phone on it.

She reached down and grabbed them. She knew that she couldn't let James see these. She unfolded the sticky note and stuck it to a page inside an old book. She tucked the scrap of paper in there too. A worn copy of *Through the Looking-Glass* that she kept on her side table. Jill had probably read that book a hundred times now, since first reading it as a kid. Her favorite.

James had no interest in books, and Jill was confident he would never find the papers hidden away in it. Above all, she knew that he couldn't ever know that she had looked at his phone. He would beat the shit out of her if he found out.

But Jill had an idea, and it was written on that small sticky note. A name and an address. It was an idea that could make the risk worth it—an idea that could change things for the better. Something life changing. She took her idea with her to her dreams as she fell asleep.

Chapter 4 – Ice Cold.

James woke Jill up when he came home later that morning.

Peeking out of her half-opened eyes, she looked out the window at what appeared to be dawn. Jill guessed it was about 7 a.m.

"Hey!" James said, as he walked over to the bed.

"Hey!" Jill replied, looking at her smiling, handsome lover. He stood in front of her next to their bed; his clothes were soaked with rain.

James reached out and touched Jill's face. His hands were ice-cold.

"What the hell?!" she exclaimed, quickly sitting up. "You are freezing!"

"What?! I'm fine," James said, still smiling vacantly.

He was definitely high; Jill just didn't know what he was high on.

"We need to get you out of these wet clothes and into something warm," she insisted, climbing out of bed. "You're going to get sick."

James stood at the foot of the bed and watched Jill with a drug-induced, childlike wonder.

She grabbed a pair of sweatpants and the most comfortable tee shirt she could find.

Jill slowly undressed the attractive, blue-eyed man, and then helped him into the dry clothes. She ran a soft, dry towel through his wet, golden-blonde hair, drying it as much as possible.

Jill had James get into bed, where she curled up next to him, trying to warm his chilled body.

"Where were you?" Jill asked quietly.

"Oh, out by Fourth Street," he said. "I know a guy out there." James yawned.

"What were you doing there?"

James stared blankly. No response.

"So...well...I have to work tonight. I picked up a shift. I need to make some extra money," Jill said, not telling James what she was really doing.

"I'm going to go get my hair done before I go in. A woman at work is going to do it for free," she added.

James nodded. He happily went along with everything she said; he was completely complacent.

He was sound asleep within minutes. Jill lay awake in bed next to her cold lover.

Something had to change.

Jill eventually fell asleep and didn't wake again until midafternoon. James was gone. She hadn't even heard him or felt him move at all during the night.

She grabbed her phone. 'Where are you, babe?' she texted her beloved James. She waited a few minutes but sadly got no reply.

Jill got up and made lunch—a cheap bowl of macaroni and cheese from a cardboard box. She watched the local news while she ate. Kitty was curled up in her lap, on the couch, the whole time.

She sat and folded the laundry that had still been sitting there in a pile from a previous trip to the laundromat. Jill had been very busy ever since. She put everything away along with the folded clothes from yesterday.

Everything was quiet. Jill enjoyed the peacefulness of the moment. She wanted to read a book.

Jill didn't have many books of her own, so reading options were limited. She only rarely borrowed books from the library now. When she used to, they always seemed to disappear, leaving her owing money to replace them—money she didn't have.

Jill went to the couple's small bedroom and grabbed one of the few, if not the only, possessions she cared about—her old copy of *Through the Looking-Glass* that sat on the night stand next to her side of the bed.

The book had belonged to her mother when she was a girl. Her mother had given it to Jill before she died. It was the only thing of her mother's that she still had left.

Jill opened her favorite book and started from page one. She quickly lost herself in the story, getting swept away like she always did. Of course, Kitty curled up next to her and purred softly like *he* always did.

Halfway through the book, she realized that she had lost track of time. She stopped where she was, marking the page with the secret piece of loose scrap paper, so that it was still hidden from James. She set the book down where it belonged, next to her side of the bed, and then she got ready for the evening.

She dressed as if she was going to work at the bar, secretly tucking a slinky black dress and red high heels into her bag.

Jill headed out to her friend's place to get a free haircut. She met the woman at the front door of her small studio apartment.

The place was old and rundown but cozy and had a warmth that made up for the distressed cosmetics. Paint peeled off the walls, the faucet never stopped dripping, and the floors were beat-up. However, despite the rough appearance, it still felt safe and comfortable to Jill.

Jill sat on a dining room chair in the kitchen while the nice, older woman brushed and then cut her hair.

The friendly woman's name was Abina. She was a beautiful, older African American woman who had been born on a Tuesday, about fifty years ago.

The two women chatted and laughed. They talked about everything from current events to lost lovers. It wasn't just a haircut; it was therapy. Abina was the only person that Jill had ever considered a true, honest friend whom she actually trusted.

"I *love* it! Thanks for everything!" Jill said to Abina after she finished drying her freshly washed hair. "I promise when I get some extra money, I'm going to tip you."

"Oh don't worry about it, dear! You already helped me, and that's enough. Look, I don't want to work at a bar anymore; I want to cut hair again. You helped give me some practice that I need to get the hell out of there," the woman said with a beautiful smile.

"Well, you did a really good job with the cut! You don't realize it but you helped me too, so thank you," Jill replied gratefully.

"Well then, we are even now, aren't we?" Abina said with a wink.

Jill nodded, not really wanting to agree. She hated taking handouts, but she saw her point.

She changed out of her bar clothes and into the slinky black dress and red high heels that she had tucked away in her bag.

"Well, I've got to run. Thanks again!" Jill admired her now shoulder-length hair in the mirror one last time.

"You're welcome, love," the kind woman said.

Jill left and started walking. It was a cool, breezy evening. She walked as far as she could and then caught a cab to her destination. She didn't have much money, so the shorter the cab ride, the better.

Jill hoped that everything would work out for her tonight.

Chapter 5 – A "Not So Private" Party.

Arriving at her destination, Jill walked up to the beautiful, extravagantly decorated home.

The property was gated, but luckily, the gate had been left open for the evening's festivities.

The large, mansion-type home sat on beautifully manicured landscape and was adorned with very expensive, exotic décor.

Jill definitely did not fit in here, but tonight she was going to try her best; after all, pretending was one of the few things she was good at.

Jill was greeted by the host—a well-dressed man in his late thirties.

"Hi! I'm glad you could make it. Welcome to our home. I'm Daniel. Mark, my partner, is around here somewhere," the gentleman introduced himself.

"You look stunning! Those shoes are amazing on you!" the host added.

"Thank you. Your home is so beautiful," Jill said, still in awe at the visually stunning decor. She admired the expensive lifestyle that she didn't get to experience very often.

"Thank you. That's because of Mark; he's great at decorating. Anyway, please make yourself at home. If you need to leave your purse or anything, we are using this bedroom as a coatroom," Daniel said, pointing toward an open door as they passed. He ushered her through the large, open kitchen and toward the back of the house.

The large glass doors opened onto the most amazing pool Jill had ever seen. She could see bodies in the pool, distorted as they stood behind the wall of smooth, rushing water falling from above.

"The bar is out there by the pool. Have fun!" the host said with a wink. "I have a few things I need to go do, if you'll excuse me."

"Of course! Thank you so much!" Jill responded sincerely.

Jill walked out to the bar and got a drink. She looked at all the faces of the people outside. Everyone was laughing and chatting, some already more drunk than others. Like a fly on the wall, she quietly watched. She didn't know anyone at all. Even Daniel, the host, was a total stranger.

She looked at all the guests as she sipped her drink. She quietly watched the wealthy people as they discussed things that she couldn't even comprehend, like stock prices, college funds, and fine art.

Finally, after about an hour of watching…Jill saw him—the man she wanted to go home with. The man she was there for. He was talking with a couple at the edge of the steaming heated pool. Dressed in an outfit that Jill knew cost more than she could probably make in one week, the stylish but personable man was very intimidating.

The mysterious man's messy brown hair blew in the breeze as he laughed at something the woman he was talking to said. His bright blue eyes caught Jill's for a split second. Jill sighed. She thought he was gorgeous, and more so in person than she had expected. The pictures she had seen online hadn't done him justice.

In the distance, the couple finished talking with him and excused themselves to get another drink.

"Well, here goes nothing," Jill said to herself quietly, as she smoothed out her slinky black dress.

Jill walked over to the handsome, intriguing stranger, who was now standing alone.

"It's a beautiful night, isn't it?" she said, breaking the ice with a cheap, awkwardly presented line.

"It is," he replied with a nod and a warm smile that made Jill melt.

"Hi, I'm Bern. Have we met?" the handsome artist asked.

"No, but I'm a fan of your art. My name is Alice," she said, shaking Bern's hand.

"Nice to meet you, Alice. You want to go with me to get another drink?" he asked.

"Sure," Jill answered nervously. She knew she could use something stronger to settle her nerves.

Jill didn't really know too much about Bern's art, she had heard of him and seen his work, she knew she liked it and that was about it. Anything else she knew, was from researching online, after recognizing his name on James' phone. Through the use of social media, it was easy to find where he would be tonight. The address she had written on the sticky note, hidden in a book, that lay next to her side of the bed. A private pool party? No problem.

"So, Alice, tell me about yourself," Bern said, as they waited for their drinks.

Jill was definitely Bern's type—tall, curvy, beautiful, and sexy. Her hair was cut differently than it had been a few hours ago. It was now shoulder-length and had been dyed blonde, something she tried to do when she knew she was going to have to strip. It ensured fewer people possibly recognizing her when she was done. Jill always dyed it back to her usual brown as soon as she could. It had become part of something like her unfortunate alter ego—a routine step in the vicious, secret cycle of stripping. This was Alice.

Bern and Jill talked for a while, and the conversation flowed effortlessly. After another drink, Jill felt very comfortable.

"Let's get in the pool," she said. "I'm wearing my suit under my dress." She pulled the dress off her shoulder to reveal the strap of a red bikini top.

The beautiful heated pool was lined with natural stone and looked like a private lagoon out of a movie. Brilliant blue water fell from the top of a large cave.

"Okay, I need to go out to my car and get my suit. You want to come with me?" he asked.

"Sure!" Jill replied excitedly.

They walked out of the house and over to the black Porsche convertible parked out front. Jill admired the car—her intended ride back to this man's place later tonight.

Bern reached in the backseat and grabbed a pair of shorts and a towel.

"I go to parties like this a lot, so I'm always prepared," he said with a grin.

The couple walked back through the magnificent home and out to the oasis-like pool.

"Let me go get my suit on," Bern said, as he watched Alice slide the dress over her head, leaving nothing but a skimpy red bikini and matching red high heels.

Bern quickly got his suit on in the bathroom and came back out to find Alice already in the pool with a fresh drink in her hand. He set his clothes down on a chair, grabbed his drink, and joined her in the water.

"I really love your artwork; I know I said that already but..." Jill said, instantly wondering if the additional compliment was too corny.

"Thank you so much. I like your tattoos. It's rare to find attractive tattoos on such a sexy body," Bern commented. "What do you do, Alice?"

"I'm a...secretary," Jill said hesitantly, feeling a little inadequate in relation to the very successful artist with whom she was flirting.

"Hmmm...a sexy, tattooed secretary. I like it. You must be every guy's fantasy," he said, with a contrasting chauvinistic yet gentlemanly smile that made Jill melt.

"Oh stop," she blushed. "I love your tattoos too!" she said, shifting the focus off of herself as she slowly ran her fingers down his inked arm.

"Do you live in the city?" Bern asked.

"Yeah, down by First and Amistad," Jill answered.

"Oh, I know that area. I actually need to go over there later this week for some art supplies," Bern said, as he thought about the colors he needed to get in order to finish a large piece he was working on.

"Oh, I know the place then. The art store on the corner by the coffee shop with that little grocery store across the street," Jill said with familiarity.

"Yep, I go there all the time," Bern responded.

"Well, you should let me know the next time. I'm usually around." Jill smiled enticingly.

"I'll probably be down there sometime Monday morning," Bern noted.

The couple continued to flirt for hours. It was mesmerizing. It was seductive.

"If you'll excuse me, I really need to use the bathroom," Jill said, interrupting the nightlong, flirtatious conversation.

"Of course. I'll be right here when you get back," Bern replied.

He watched the drops of crystal water glide sensually down the back of the blonde woman's skin as she ascended the pool stairs. The soft light and reflection of the water danced along her curves, accentuating them seductively. Bern wanted to feel those curves. He wanted to taste them.

As Alice walked away, Bern slowly followed her out of the pool, being cautious to hide how excited the blonde bombshell had gotten him. He checked his phone, which he had left siting on his towel. He saw ten missed calls and twenty-five new messages in the last fifteen minutes; they were all from his best friend, Anna.

'Hey I'm still stuck here. It's a bad part of town. I need help! PLEASE!!!' the most recent, desperate message from Anna read.

She had gotten a flat tire in a bad part of the city. She was very bookish and not good with tools. Bern knew that she definitely couldn't change a tire by herself.

'I'm on my way!' He replied, seeing that she had already sent the address of the intersection about twenty messages earlier.

Bern rushed toward the front door with a towel around his waist and dry clothes in his hand, grabbing the host's attention on his way.

"Can I ask you a favor? If a hot blonde named Alice is looking for me, can you give her my number and tell her I'm sorry, I had an emergency?"

"Sure thing. Are you okay?" Daniel asked with concern.

"Yeah, I have just got to run. Thanks, buddy! Give me a call sometime. We can go to the shooting range or something," Bern said with a nod.

"Will do. Drive safe!" Daniel replied.

Bern got in his jet-black Porsche and put the address in the car's GPS. The dark, classy automobile sped away at breakneck speed, with a push of Bern's wet, bare foot on the cold, metal, gas pedal.

He quickly got dressed at a long red light, and then he called Anna.

"Hey! I'm on my way!" he said when she answered.

"Thank God! Where have you been?!" she asked, relieved to finally hear his voice.

"Sorry, I was caught up. But I'll be there in like five minutes."

"Stay on the phone with me," Anna said.

"Okay."

Bern and Anna talked while he drove across town.

"What did you do—sit in the car with the doors locked the whole time?" he asked with a grin that seemed to jump through the phone.

"Yes. What was I supposed to do? Stop laughing!" Anna replied.

"Okay, I'm here."

Bern pulled up to the intersection and saw Anna's car stopped ahead, pulled off to the side with the hazard lights on.

Bern pulled up behind her. Anna opened the passenger door.

"Thank you so much!" she said, as she got into his car. "Yuck, this is wet'" Anna said as she threw the wet towel, from the passenger's seat, onto the back floor.

"Let's just leave your car here. I will call my roadside assistance company. They will pick up the keys from us, and then come out, fix the tire, and deliver the car to your door. It will be waiting for you in the morning," Bern said.

"Seriously?"

"Yep!" Bern answered, as the couple sped away.

Back at the party, Jill came out of the bathroom to find Bern, and all his stuff, gone. Looking around, she saw no sign of him. She grabbed her purse and hastily walked through the house and out to the front.

"Hey, Alice!" the host called, trying to get her attention as he saw her walking out.

Jill didn't respond to the alias.

In front of the house she found one missing, sexy, black Porsche, and only faint, black tire marks where it had been parked.

"Damn it!" she said, frustrated. She knew she didn't have enough money for the taxi ride home.

"Goddamn it! Fuck that guy!" Jill said, stomping on the ground, still barefoot. Her tall red heels still sat in the back by the beautiful, romantic pool.

She walked back into the house. She needed to find a ride home or borrow some money for a cab.

Jill wanted to cry.

She couldn't help but notice the first guest bedroom that she passed—the room that the host had pointed out was for the wealthy guests to use as a coatroom.

She walked into the room, making sure no one saw her. Inside the dimly lit room, Jill saw a row of suit jackets hanging on a coatrack and a couple purses lying on the bed. Jill grabbed the nicest-looking purse and quickly went into the attached bathroom, locking the door behind her. She quickly dug through the expensive purse and found forty-five dollars and a prescription bottle with a couple pills in it. It was enough money to get her home, and hopefully the pills were something she could give James to calm him down.

Jill nonchalantly threw the purse back down on the bed and walked out of the coatroom with the stolen cash and drugs now hidden in her own purse.

"Hey, are you Alice?" Daniel asked, as he came around the corner, startling the petty thief.

"No, I'm Jill," she responded in haste, without thinking.

"Oh, I'm sorry. I'm looking for someone else," he said, and then walked away.

Jill called a cab from the house phone and waited out front.

On the ride home, she admitted to herself that she truly found Bern charming and alluring. She wished that the extravagant world she left behind could be her own, even for just a day.

But, sadly it wasn't, and she knew that it probably never would be. Jill knew she was still going to have to strip to pay the bills and to get enough money for the drugs James needed.

It was back to reality...for Alice. She had to go home to her own bedroom. Just like in the book, tonight she got to see Wonderland for a few hours, and it left her with a broken heart.

The night didn't go the way Jill had hoped.

When she finally got home, James wasn't there. It was becoming almost routine; he was either out on a psychotic journey or he was trying to score something to calm his mind down.

Jill watched her reflection in the mirror as she took the slinky black dress off and let it slide to the floor. The red bikini she had on for the pool party was still wet.

She slid the bottoms down her long legs and then slowly untied the top. Goose bumps quickly spread across her gorgeous body. The red suit now sat in a damp pile on the floor. This left the seductive blonde standing naked and alone. Jill looked at the reflection of a woman whom she didn't feel like she recognized. Now she looked like someone else. She had even spent the whole night pretending to be someone else. She looked at her reflection and wished she saw a normal, average woman looking back at her.

Jill climbed into the couple's cold, small bed and curled up by herself. She went to sleep alone again, wondering where James was.

Chapter 6 – Growing Up Fucked Up.

Jill awoke to the sound of James laughing, almost maniacally.

She opened her gentle, hazel eyes to see him through the bedroom doorway, sitting on the couch, watching their small color television.

"What are...you doing?" she sleepily mumbled as she rubbed her eyes.

"Watching TV," he replied, looking over at her like a kid watching Saturday morning cartoons in the early 80's.

"What are you watching?" Jill asked, as she slowly walked into the room, yawning.

"Hey, you dyed your hair again. I bet it only lasts a week. Remember every other time you've dyed it blonde? You never keep it." James pointed out the truth. As soon as she didn't need to strip anymore, Jill always dyed it back to brown.

"Yeah, I just get bored with it quickly. I couldn't keep it this way for too long, " Jill said, now thinking of the past couple times she had dyed it to strip.

"Let's watch that cartoon from when we were kids. What was it called...where they solved mysteries?" James asked.

"I don't remember, it's too early," Jill said, laughing sleepily.

James eventually found the cartoon. It was exactly how they remembered it as kids. Jill curled up next to him on the couch. Having the normal James back was like a drug to her. Jill felt high. She would do anything for this high—even strip.

She didn't know what James was on. But she knew that she didn't feel threatened. She didn't feel like she was about to be unpredictably beaten at any second. This was the James she loved; he was back for a short period of time.

They sat and watched the cartoon gang and their dog solve the mystery. Of course, it was Old Man Jenkins in the ghoul costume. It usually was.

Jill slept peacefully until the twitch of James' body, along with a loud laugh, woke her up.

"Hey. What are you doing?" she said with a smile.

"Watching a documentary about Bonnie and Clyde," James said. "It's pretty sick."

"Why were you laughing so hard?" she asked curiously.

"Oh, some stupid commercial." he laughed a little more.

James seemed wide awake and on edge—a different James from the one Jill had fallen asleep with. Her high was over...reality was back...she was going to need a fix soon.

Jill planned on stripping tonight. She should be able to make enough money for one month's worth of James' prescriptions, and then a couple more nights to save for the next couple refills. To her, degrading her body in front of sweaty, sloppy, horny men was worth it for a high that lasted a whole month. Just like a junky, James was her drug.

"Did you know that Bonnie's last name was Parker? I have a cousin named Parker. I mean, it's his first name, but I still thought it was cool."

"I didn't know that. Parker, I like that," Jill said.

James turned the volume up on the TV, and they watched the rest of the documentary together.

'...Before the officers could draw their guns, they were shot dead by bullets fired by the wanted lovers...Bonnie and Clyde.'

"Can you imagine?! That's nuts!" Jill exclaimed. "I would love to live like that! Always on the run. So much excitement! I couldn't kill anybody though. Not on purpose anyway."

"I think I could," James said, nodding. "I mean, even with all the murder and robbery. You just have to detach yourself from all that. You have to be cold-blooded," James said, sounding more serious than he ever had.

"I mean, minus all the murder and robbery... every day would be an adventure," Jill said, hoping that James was kidding, but knowing deep down inside that he probably wasn't.

James sat on the edge of their couch, wearing his old, ripped jeans and a plain, white undershirt. He lit the second half of a cheap cigarette he had extinguished earlier and puffed the thick, white smoke.

"Yeah. Fuck people though, you know. People don't care about you. Why should you care about them? I think that shit would be easy. So what, another asshole died a little earlier than he was supposed to? He was headed there anyway, just like everyone else!" His stare felt like it was piercing into Jill like a sharp knife.

"Are you really that cold?" Jill instantly regretted asking the question.

"You know I am, baby...I told you...no one cares, so why should I?" the handsome, apathetic loser said, as he brushed his cold hand down her warm cheek.

His ice-cold touch sent shivers across Jill's entire body.

"Yeah, you're right. No one cares," Jill said, as she looked away from James and stared out the window.

Jill had a hard time when James was off his medication. He was unpredictable and difficult to be around, especially when his dark side surfaced.

When James' mind took him to that place, he became a different person. Cruel and violent, he was a man whom Jill loathed—a man she hated and feared.

James' moods went from deep depression to severe mania. When he was not on medication, he was mostly on the maniacal end of the spectrum. James' mania was angry and violent. Life was hell when he was like this.

The couple always had a hard time affording James' medication. It cost so much money, but it was the only way life was tolerable for them. Since Jill had a criminal record, she was unable to get most government assistance. She had to pay for everything without any other help at all.

The bar Jill worked at had been unusually slow for the past couple of months, which caused Jill's income to be cut in half. This put her under twice the pressure when it came to paying the bills.

On top of that, James seemed to be getting worse—angrier and more violent. Jill had been trying to get more shifts at work and had even applied for a second job at some other places. Unfortunately, she hadn't found anything yet.

Jill would do anything to get James back on his medication. She just needed money for another month.

If she had to go strip for a few nights again, then she'd do it if that's what it was going to take—anything for her lover and best friend.

"Oh shit! I forgot! I got these for you!" Jill said, grabbing her purse off the floor. She grabbed the prescription bottle that she had taken from the designer purse at the party. She got the two pills out and gave them to James, who swallowed the pills without question.

Jill knew she would be high again soon.

"Hey, I never told you the details of the text message," James said. Just the act of taking the drugs again made him start to lighten up almost immediately.

"Well…some random guy contacted me. He said he knew about a secret government lab right here in the city," James started. "I have talked to him on the phone a few times now."

"Who is it?" Jill inquired.

"He didn't give me his name," James said, yawning.

"And you believe him?" Jill asked skeptically.

"Why not? It's worth looking into. Anyway, we may not have to go to Boston now. Here is what we have...a few names to look at: David Oxford, Anna Smith, and Bern Andrews."

He showed Jill pictures on his phone. She acted surprised by the information.

"Well, who are they?" Jill asked, playing dumb, knowing that James would be pissed off if he found out that she already knew about any of this. He would absolutely kill her if he knew she had already done research on Bern and tracked him to a party for her own agenda, her secret reasons.

"I'm not sure. I see these two together often. I don't know though; they don't seem like they're dating. He is really the only other person I see her with." James was starting to act groggy.

"What do you mean, you 'see them together'?" she inquired, lowering her eyebrows.

"I have been following these people around," James admitted proudly.

"Are you stupid?! James, that is so risky! Is that where you have been disappearing to? Why didn't you tell me?" Jill questioned angrily.

"I'm not stupid, Jill!" James said quietly in a slightly angry but still melancholy tone.

"If you don't need me around, just tell me. It would make my life a lot easier." Jill regretted her words the moment they came out of her mouth. Luckily, the pills had lulled James into a complacent state of mind. If he hadn't taken the pills, he would have beaten her ass in a heartbeat for saying something like that.

"Whatever. You aren't going anywhere."

Jill ignored him.

"This is perfect, I'll take him," she said, confidently pointing to Bern's picture on James' phone.

"What?! No way!" James protested, although not very convincingly.

"Yeah! Look at him! He looks so cocky, like an arrogant prick. He will be a piece of cake," Jill said. "I can have that guy eating out of my hand in no time. If he knows anything, I will get him to tell me," Jill insisted.

She looked at Bern's picture again, noting how handsome he appeared. She thought about the time they spent flirting and the way the mysterious artist had made her feel.

"I'll just follow him and see if he knows anything. I'll follow him to a bar or something and just start talking to him," she said nonchalantly. "I need an alias. Okay...I got it. I'll be...Alice," Jill said, as if she had just invented the character. She glanced at the treasured old book on the table next to her side of the bed and smiled. 'Bern Andrews,' a small scrap of paper and a sticky note inside the book read. One with a phone number jotted down from James phone. The other with an address that Jill found through social media. They secretly marked the story at about the middle.

"Alice...seriously?! Like a mom from the1970s who sells plastic containers at parties and bakes cookies...kind of Alice?" James said with a slow, drugged laugh.

"No! Like...*Alice in Wonderland* Alice!" Jill pointed to the book on the nightstand.

James reached over and picked up the special book.

What the fuck? Jill thought. *All these years and he has never once picked that book up!*

Jill stared nervously as James flipped through the pages. She closely watched for the middle of the book, where the secret notes were, to pass by. Suddenly, her heart stopped as a small, familiar scrap of paper fluttered out of the book and down onto the bed, next to her unpredictably, unstable lover.

'Bern Andrews' it read in Jill's beautiful handwriting, along with his phone number.

She held her breath as she watched James finish flipping through the pages of the old, beloved book— the last place she thought he would never find the secret notes. Lucky for her she only had the scrap of paper to worry about. The sticky note had stayed stuck in the book.

She stared fearfully, at the scrap of paper, siting in plain sight. She quickly started thinking of an alibi; what was she going to say? How the hell was she going to get out of this one?

"Oh...Alice...in Wonderland..." Was the last thing James said, as he trailed off to sleep, the book slowly falling from his hands as he started to snore.

Jill cautiously reached over and grabbed the scrap of paper, her secret note that threatened her physical wellbeing. She took the secret to their bathroom and held it over the toilet; she didn't need this one anymore.

Jill grabbed James' lighter from the counter and lit the note with a flick and a spark. She watched the flames quickly consume the paper and the ashes fall into the water below. Jill let out a deep sigh of relief.

Jill and James had originally met in elementary school. They were the two obvious problem children in their 5th-grade class, so they naturally gravitated toward each other. The pair of troubled youth quickly became inseparable; that is, until Jill's parents moved across the country at the beginning of her second year of high school. This forcibly separated the two, and they eventually lost contact as the years slowly passed by.

As pre-teens, they had both shared the bond of being raised in the same dysfunctional, broken-home type of background. Although their families' situations were different, the two adolescents had an obvious connection.

Jill's father, when he was around, was physically and emotionally abusive to both Jill and her mother, driving the family apart. His angry focus on Jill only escalated as she got older. The heightened abuse drove Jill to drop out of school and run away from home at the age of seventeen.

James, on the other hand, didn't know who his father was. He was raised solely by his mother, a nearly homeless junkie who left James alone to fend for himself at a very young age.

He remembered nights when his mother would bring different strange men home, and he remembered the nights that she didn't come home at all. Every one of those horrible nights unknowingly strengthened the demon inside the impressionable young man.

An unacknowledged mental illness that, over time, only got worse.

Jill and James eventually reunited in their late twenties at a homeless shelter in the city. Neither had really gone anywhere in life. The troubled couple quickly let drug abuse take over their lives; they lost control of everything and lived day to day, just to get high. They spent as much time getting high as they could. The rest of the time they were either sleeping or looking for more drugs for their next high. The couple did what they had to do to survive, rummaging through unlocked cars, snatching purses, stealing credit cards...

They were perfect for each other.

This vicious drug-abuse cycle lasted a long enough time that Jill was surprised every day when she woke up that she was still alive. She was even more surprised every day when James also woke up.

Even just being alive seemed to defy all odds.

A couple of years ago, however, Jill got sick of the junky lifestyle and forced them both to change. It was triggered not solely by the despair she endured daily, but also by James' third overdose. Clinically, he had died two times, and the doctors had had to fight hard to get him back. That was finally Jill's wake-up call.

A memory Jill would never forget was holding her overdosed lover in her arms as he foamed at the mouth and convulsed violently. She remembered sitting on the floor of the dirty, public subway bathroom, as she helplessly watched James dying. She promised that day that if her lover lived, she was going to make changes. Luckily, someone had called the paramedics, and they had arrived in time to save him with a Narcan injection, that reversed the heroin overdose, and a lifesaving trip to the emergency room.

As horrible as her life was, she couldn't imagine it without James by her side. She couldn't imagine going through this painful life alone. He was her best friend and her worst enemy all in one.

They had both gotten clean and stayed clean—at least as clean as their troubled minds, still scarred from their youth, were going to allow them to get and allow them to stay.

James currently had the couple immersed in an underground movement—a movement against government control. It started innocently but had now turned into farfetched conspiracy theories about government mind control. They had been to rally after rally and protest after protest, and it was really trying on them as a couple; but their involvement kept James focused on something other than drugs, and this was why Jill went along with it all.

Word was spreading about some documents that had been leaked out of a secret government facility in Boston, and now James wanted them to go there. He was obsessed with *'finding the truth'* as he called it.

"Maybe we won't need to go to Boston now," Jill remembered James saying earlier.

"That's what the fight was about! Fuck!" Jill said to herself, reliving the memory of the other morning when she couldn't remember why James was mad at her.

"I don't want to go to Boston. We can't afford to go to Boston," Jill protested. "We can't just go there and have no income!"

"But this is it! We are sitting on the verge of something huge," James said passionately. "We are part of history. Everything is going to change soon. The people are going to take control. It will be our country again." The sober James spoke very persuasively.

"Okay, I know. I get it...but we still fucking need to pay the electric bill and the rent. Going to Boston doesn't pay the bills. This is such a stupid argument," Jill said in an irritated tone.

This, of course, pissed James off. This is why he was mad the other morning. Now she remembered.

Sometimes Jill got fed up with the whole conspiracy theory talk that James always went on about. However, it consumed his mind and kept him busy. He was always looking for new information. As old as it got sometimes, though, she knew that without this focus, James would be a bored junky again in just a matter of days. Jill usually listened, but now it was becoming more serious, with irrational thoughts of going to another state. Jill knew that this would pull them away from what little stability she had worked so hard to achieve for them, with little help from James.

Jill just wanted to enjoy life. She knew nothing they could do was going to change anything anyway. Two high-school dropouts with a mental illness were never going to make a difference in the world.

The bonus that Jill saw in even going along with this new lead was to end the talk about going to Boston. If James had something to look for here, they could stay while she continued to get their lives together. Because of this, Jill encouraged the local inquiries no matter how crazy they seemed.

Jill fueled the proverbial fire.

Chapter 7 – The Rabbit Hole.

Jill was dreading getting ready for work tonight. She hated stripping.

She knew, though, that things were going to get better. She could feel it. Everything was going to turn around soon.

She packed her bag and headed to work. She planned on using all the money she made tonight for James' prescriptions.

Jill walked into the dark, loud strip club. She hated the people, she hated the sounds, and she hated the smell. She just wanted to get this night over with.

"Hey, lovely! Glad to see you made it out tonight!" the club manager said. "You saw the sign out front?"

"Yeah," Jill said, trying her best to fake a genuine-looking smile.

She went to the back room and started getting ready. She took her clothes off and put her costume on—a sexy, adult version of Alice from *Alice in Wonderland*.

Jill had been clean for almost five years, except when it came to stripping. She had one hell of a hard time getting naked in front of strange men when she was sober.

She didn't count this against her sobriety though. Luckily, she had now become a sexy, seductive version of her favorite character.

Alice snorted a small bump of cocaine that she had been hanging onto for such emergencies. The cocaine rushed through her blood and to her brain. It created a sudden surge of energy. Everything felt good. Euphoric.

With her brain's neurotransmitters impacted by the white powder, stripping was now a much more tolerable act. Jill heard her song start, and then the DJ made the introduction.

"Welcome our guest star to the stage tonight! If you have ever had a rare chance to see her perform, consider yourself lucky. The beautifully seductive 'Miss Wonderland'."

Jill took a deep breath...

She hit the dark stage with the confidence of Alice, scattering a cheap deck of playing cards in front of her as she walked. The hearts, diamonds, clubs, and spades spread across the floor. Black and red. The less-than-perfect gentlemen cheered with excitement.

Alice's costume was a risqué blue-and-white dress that was short enough to see her ass peeking out of the bottom edge. Up top, the dress was low-cut and showed a large amount of cleavage. Jill's large, perky breasts bounced as she danced in the sexy outfit.

She was wearing perfectly themed white stockings with red hearts and black spades down the outside seam. A white-and-blue, ruffled bow was tied on top of her head. Her feet were perched inside of very tall, sexy black stilettos.

She was Alice—her unfortunate, cocaine driven, blonde alter ego that kept Jill from being the one who had to strip. Alice did the dirty work that Jill couldn't.

She slowly slid the skimpy dress off her shoulders, letting the blue-and-white fabric fall to the stage floor.

Alice was left dancing in a lacy white bra and matching lace white thong. She danced on the stage, full of coke-fueled energy. The sweat glistened on her body, under the hot lights.

She looked incredible, like a shimmering vixen.

The men in the club watched in wonderment and lust.

Alice slid the white lacy bra off, setting her voluptuous breasts free as her body continued to move seductively to the music. She sparkled provocatively under the multicolored lights.

"Eat me! Drink me!" a drunk man said loudly, holding out a ten-dollar bill.

"Maybe later," Alice said with a wink, as she let the man tuck the green paper into her stocking.

She pulled a playing card out from a special deck, gave it a kiss, and then threw it at the man. The Ace of Spades.

Alice always had another special deck of cards tucked into the elastic of her stocking. Each card was signed 'Love, Alice' and had a stick heart drawn on it. She herself had been calling them *stick hearts* ever since she heard someone at the bar, where she worked, call them that.

When a guy gave her a large amount of money, she would pull a signed card out, kiss the face, and throw it at the man. Most of the regulars knew about it, and they loved it.

By the end of the night, it would always turn into a contest to see who got the most cards or the best hand. Those signed cards made Alice big money.

"I want to see your rabbit hole!" another man said, as she got closer so he could stuff money into the elastic of her sheer white socking.

Alice smiled and playfully said, in a way almost reminiscent of Marilyn Monroe, "I bet you do, but what kind of girl do you think I am?"

Alice imagined that the card in her hand was a knife. She flicked her wrist, sending the spinning knife flying toward the man. The blade hit the man in his neck, just below his double chin. The sharp knife slit his throat wide open with an extremely clean slice, sending a rush of blood spilling down his chest and into a pool on the floor.

Alice glared intensely as the playing card bounced off the man's throat and landed on the table in front of him. 'Love, Alice' it read, the face still moist from the kiss of her wet lips.

Alice grinned and looked around for the next payout.

The dark thought made it apparent that the high from the coke was wearing off. The come-down was usually a horrible, angry time for her. Luckily, her last song was ending just in time.

Alice finished dancing and headed backstage. Realizing that she didn't have any more coke, she quickly locked most of her money in the locker, threw her clothes on, and went to see the manager. She had put on a big, red, hooded sweatshirt, pulling the hood up so the lewd crowd wouldn't recognize her.

"My usual, Jill said," peering from under the oversized red hood, past her platinum, blonde hair. She slipped the large man some cash.

"Good show," he said, as he handed Jill a small bag of white powder.

"Thanks," Jill said, rushing back toward the backstage dressing room without another word.

"No, thank *you!*" the manager said, as he lustfully watched her walk away.

Jill got to the back room and quickly snorted some of the white powder from the small bag. She knew she had to go back out on stage at least one more time and be Alice again, just to make the night worth it.

Jill danced five sets of songs as Alice, each song fueled by more and more cocaine. Exhausted, she finally finished her last dance. She felt not only tired but also dirty. She was thankful to be headed home for a warm shower and to a soft bed. Jill got dressed and started walking home, or at least as far as she could get.

'Miss Alice Wonderland appearing this week!' the sign behind Jill, now in the distance, read as she walked away from the strip club. She had made enough money for another month of James' prescription, even after paying the rent and the other bills.

Life was going to be okay again.

Jill walked down the street happy, both that it was over and also to finally have the money that she desperately needed.

Turning the corner quickly onto Fourth Street, Jill ran into a tall man in a long coat. They bumped shoulders, spinning Jill sideways.

"Oh I'm so sorry!" Jill said, as her face turned red from embarrassment.

"Oh no! I'm sorry, it was my fault. I saw you walking and wanted to stop you," the man replied. "I wanted to say thank you!" the neat bearded man quickly added.

"For what?" Jill questioned.

"Telling me about that shelter. They are really helping me."

"Oh! I'm so glad to hear that," Jill said, as she now recognized the changed man. He was now wearing cleaner clothes, and he had even gotten a haircut at the shelter. Jill got out the money she had made from stripping, and she handed the man, whom she now recognized as Jerry, forty-five dollars.

"Here, I owe this to somebody, but I can't pay them back, so I am paying it back to you." Jill referred to the stolen money from the coatroom purse at the pool party.

"Thank you so much!" he said with a suddenly brighter tone. Things really were finally getting better for him.

Jill stood and looked into the eyes of someone who honestly cared. A cleaner-than-before, but still messy, bearded, kind, caring homeless man named Jerry.

"Don't give up! I was like you. That shelter helped me," Jill said reassuringly.

"Thanks again," the man said, as Jill walked away with a big smile on her face.

It was time to go home.

But first, she quickly stopped by the pharmacy and paid for one month of James' prescription drugs.

Stripping tonight was worth these three small prescription bottles.

Of course, James wasn't home when Jill got there, so she took the prescription bottles and put them on the bathroom counter along with a note that read, 'I got these for you! ~Love, Jill.'

Jill fell asleep quickly to the happy thoughts of James finally being back on his medication.

Her life would be somewhat normal again soon.

Chapter 8 – A Loaf of Bread.

Jill woke up late Tuesday morning. She felt like a worn-out stripper after a long night.

She looked in the bed next to her. James' spot was cold and empty.

"Last night was hell..." she said in a high pitched voice to Kitty, who was laying on her legs. "How was your night?" She rubbed the loving cats face.

She sat up and stretched her arms. Kitty jumped down and ran to the kitchen, telling Jill he was hungry.

Jill covered her face with her hands. The last thing she wanted to do was strip...again...tonight.

She thought of one last thing that might keep from having to strip later this evening. She decided it was worth a shot, so she got up out of bed, fed Kitty then she got all dressed up.

Jill wanted to look both classy and sexy at the same time. She now had on, what she thought was, the perfect outfit.

Jill ambitiously headed to the other side of the city. Purposefully driven.

She texted James. 'Hey! I'm going downtown. Where are you? Miss you!'

It was a dreary, overcast day. She needed to look as irresistible as possible, so she took the bus today, ensuring she would stay dry in her suggestive attire and perfectly applied makeup. She looked irresistibly enticing.

On the bus ride there, Jill made sure she had a marker and something to write on in her purse. She found an old playing card—the Queen of Hearts. It was a remnant of a long night of stripping that would be perfectly "spontaneous" and unforgettable.

Starting around 9 a.m., Jill hung around First and Amistad for the rest of the morning, vigilantly watching.

Then, finally, around 12:30, it happened...

A suave, brown-haired figure ducked into the corner grocery store.

Jill hurried to cross the street, keeping her eye on the front door. Once she got to the front of the store, she quietly slipped inside unnoticed.

She watched, from the opposite side of the store, as Bern grabbed a loaf of bread from the rack.

"Bern!" she exclaimed.

Jill was wearing a tight black skirt and a semi-sheer, white button-down dress shirt. Her blonde hair was up, and she had a pair of black framed glasses on her beautiful face. She was trying to pull off a sexy secretary look, just like Bern had mentioned the other night in the pool.

"Hey, Alice!" Bern said, as he watched the ravishing blonde walking toward him.

Jill swayed her curvy body as she walked in the tall, red high heels.

"I didn't get your number the other night," she said.

"Oh my God, I know! I'm so sorry! I was in a hurry to get out of there. There was an emergency, and I couldn't find you on my way out. I told Daniel to give you my number," Bern explained.

"Oh, is everything okay?" Jill asked, as she gave him a hug. She made sure she pushed her large, perky breasts into his chest so Bern could feel their softness.

"Yeah, it was just a friend that was in some trouble."

Jill saw that Bern was having trouble focusing on anything other than her perfectly luscious cleavage.

She was definitely okay with using her body when she needed to.

"You look good!" she said, winking at Bern, when he finally made eye contact again. "Here's my number." Jill used a permanent marker to finish writing on the Queen of Hearts from her purse. This was exactly why she made sure that she had them in there. "Sorry, that was the only thing I had to write on in here," she said, as she put the marker back in her purse and handed Bern the card.

"No, it's cool; I like it," he said, as he looked at the playing card, flipping it over in his fingers. The red was as red as it could be. The black was as black as it could be. Both colors were bold and vibrant, yet the dark silhouette of the queen had eyes that looked somehow, forlorn and vacant.

"You want to go to dinner Thursday night?" Jill asked, as she gently bit her bottom lip.

Hook him! Make Thursday irresistible! she thought, reminding herself that she wanted this more than she wanted to strip ever again.

"We can go back to your place afterwards," Jill added quickly, as she slowly slid her hand down his tattooed arm. She could feel Bern's tiny goose bumps.

"Sure, Thursday it is," Bern said with a noticeable, nervous quiver.

"Text me and we can make a plan," Jill said, throwing Bern the most mischievously sexy grin she could pull off.

Jill leaned over and kissed Bern on his cheek, making sure he could feel her warm, half-exposed cleavage against his bare arm.

"Bye," she whispered in his ear in a lusciously seductive tone, her soft lips gently touching the edge of his ear.

Jill walked away slowly. She knew Bern was watching, so she made sure her walk was something to look at. She swayed and bent with a deliberate, sexy strut. Jill stopped over by the cereal and pretended that she had been shopping there when Bern had walked in.

She carefully watched as Bern walked out of the grocery store. Jill laughed when she noticed that he had forgotten his loaf of bread.

"That went well," she said to herself, shrugging her shoulders.

Jill started walking home, no longer worried about getting wet. As usual, she was trying to get as close as she could before she spent money on a cab.

She heard her phone's message notification and looked at the screen. '*Pick you up at 8:30. Text me your address sometime. ;)*,' the message read, from a number that she didn't recognize.

Jill saved the number as 'Bern–the artist.'

She planned on just having him meet her at a bar for a few drinks and some food—someplace that was a good distance from where she really lived.

Jill headed home, feeling hopeful for the near future.

She looked at her phone as she walked. 'I'm home,' a message from James read. It was the first time she had heard from him all day.

She walked as far as she could and then caught a cab.

'I'm almost there,' she replied, as the cab got closer to their home.

"So…guess who I ran into today while I was out running errands?" Jill said to James as she walked in through the front door.

"Who?" James asked.

"Bern Andrews. I am meeting him for a drink Thursday night. I will find out if he knows anything."

"Great!" James said excitedly.

"How do you feel? You started taking your pills?" Jill asked, noting his changed attitude and demeanor.

"Yeah, I feel good," James answered in a daze. Hazy.

"Let's watch a movie tonight," Jill said, excited at the possibility of a normal night on the couch as a couple, thanks to the prescriptions.

"I'll rent something this afternoon. I need to run to the grocery store anyway. We don't have anything to eat, and I made good money last night. Do you want anything special? You want to go with me?" Jill asked.

"No, I'll stay here," James responded slowly, more dazed than usual.

Jill went to the store and bought a list of things for a house with no food—staples like bread, milk, and eggs, along with some luxuries like soda and ice cream.

Jill wanted to make dinner for them to celebrate— nothing too fancy or expensive…so, spaghetti it was.

Jill walked home on the beautiful, sunny late afternoon, carrying her groceries. Everything seemed more bright and happy than ever before. She could even hear the birds chirping over the usually deafening city noise.

Jill walked into their apartment vibrant, energetic, and happy.

"What the hell took you so long?!" James snapped.

Jill looked at James. He seemed irritated and on edge.

"Whoa! You haven't been taking your prescriptions I got...have you?" Jill asked. "You told me you did! I left them on the counter."

"Yeah, I have!" James snapped back.

"James, don't lie! I can tell when you don't take them. I really need you to take them every day. Please!" Jill pleaded. "I worked hard to get those drugs so you could be normal. You have no idea how hard I work for you. You don't know what I had to go through! Please!" Jill was willing to beg. Anything for that fix— that metaphorical injection of love and emotion that got her high. Love was her drug—a euphoric chemical high with no boundaries.

"Okay, okay, I'll take them!" James said, snapping back.

"What is the deal with that wet swimsuit that you left on the floor? I thought you worked the other night?" James pushed Jill for an answer. He always tried to be in control.

"I went over to a girl's house that works at the bar with me, after we closed up. We went down to the pool at her apartment. I tried to call you, but you were out all night." Jill cautiously gave the false alibi.

"Well, next time fucking tell me where you are," James said, poking his index finger hard into her chest. His fingernail dug painfully into her soft breast.

"Okay! Ouch!" Jill said, pushing his hand away.

James' hand clenched into a tight fist as he swiftly raised it high above Jill.

She closed her scared, hazel eyes and scrunched her face in preparation for her hands being too slow to block the oncoming blow.

Her hands got up to her face...then nothing...

Jill slowly opened her eyes. James had walked away without hitting her. She saw him standing in the bathroom. In his hand were three pills, one from each prescription bottle that she had filled for him. He tossed the pills in his mouth and swallowed them with a handful of water from the faucet.

"I'm sorry," James mumbled, as he walked past Jill and out of the apartment.

Jill sat on their bed. Her hazel eyes watered. Life wasn't perfect yet, but it would be soon. Jill was always optimistic.

She sat in silence and read the second half of her favorite book, *Through the Looking-Glass*, as her cat, Kitty, lay peacefully asleep on her lap. Years ago, she had secretly and thoughtfully named him the same as Alice's cat in the book.

With Kitty by her side, Jill enjoyed a short escape away from her world to an imaginary place—a place that only existed in her mind, with characters who only existed in her mind…a place she had loved ever since she'd been a little girl.

This was Jill's Wonderland.

Chapter 9 – The New Plan.

Jill had fallen asleep after finishing her book, only to be awakened by the sound of a new text message on her phone.

'Hey, I have to cancel tomorrow. I'm so sorry. Something urgent came up. What are you doing tonight?' Jill read the text on her phone aloud.

It was from 'Bern–the artist.'

'I actually don't have plans. What about you?' She sent a reply.

'I've got nothing going on. You want to grab some drinks later?' Bern responded.

'Sure.' She sent the text with a smile on her face.

Change of plans—Jill wasn't going to work at the strip club tonight. She did need to run an errand now though, so that she would be ready for what she thought would be a pretty big evening.

She texted the strip club manager. 'I'm not going to be able to work tonight, but I do need to stop by and pick up a few things. I left a white shirt there and a pair of red panties.'

'Ok, I have them here. Pick them up anytime,' he replied.

"Thank God!" Jill said with relief. Of course, she hadn't left anything at the club, but she planned on having a very fun, rewarding night tonight.

Jill headed down to the strip club. It was a beautiful day outside. The overcrowded city was bustling.

"Hi," she said to the full-time strip club manager, who was also her part-time drug dealer.

"You did great last night! You should really come in tonight," the shady man encouraged Jill.

"I can't tonight. I already had something else scheduled," Jill replied.

"So, how many white shirts and how many red panties?" the man asked.

"Just two red panties and one white shirt."

The man put two white pills, marked with red dots on them, and a small bag of white powder into an unmarked envelope. He handed it to Jill, and then she slipped him some cash.

"I'm sorry to hear you aren't going to be coming in tonight. When will you be back?" the man inquired.

"I don't know. I'm going through some really hard times right now," Jill said, absolutely not wanting to elaborate any further.

"Ha! Aren't all you girls? Isn't that why you strip?" the man said with a chuckle.

Jill reluctantly nodded, disgusted by his comment. She turned and walked away without another word.

"Give me a call anytime you leave anything here. You know I'll always have it for you," the dealer said.

"Yeah...thanks," she said, walking out the front door without looking back.

Jill wished she never had to go back into that hell ever again.

She squinted as the intensely bright sun hit her eyes. They struggled to adjust from the darkness of the dingy strip club. She had lost her sunglasses a while ago and didn't have the money to buy a new pair.

She walked in the bright afternoon sun for a few blocks and then caught the train at the nearest stop.

When she got home, she started looking through her outfits, picking out the one she thought would be found the most irresistible.

To avoid Bern trying to pick her up at her house, she wanted to get to a bar before him. She picked one a good distance from where she lived.

"You work tonight?" James asked.

"Yeah." Jill nodded. "I'll be home late. What are you going to do?" she inquired.

"I don't know. Maybe I'll do some more research on those people," James said. He was now pleasantly calm and rational.

She could tell he really had started taking the prescriptions this time. This was the James Jill was in love with. This was the man who made everything worth it. This was the man whose return she had been waiting for.

The man who took his medication.

They spent the rest of the afternoon together. Jill made an early dinner, a big bowl of spaghetti, to celebrate.

They sat and watched an old movie—one of their favorites. Jill didn't want this to ever end. She wanted more than anything to stay home tonight.

Hopefully, later tonight will pay off and make a few more months of prescriptions possible, Jill thought, always looking on the bright side of things.

Chapter 10 – A Local Bar.

Jill walked into the bar and took a seat on a tall stool far away from all the other patrons. It was 7:30.

"Whiskey on the rocks," she said to the bartender.

Jill got out her phone and texted Bern.

'Why don't you meet me at Lou's? It's a bar over by the river on 8th Street.'

Jill had picked that bar because she had never gone there, so hopefully, no one would recognize her. It was also close to Bern's place and not near where he thought she lived. Jill had planned this as a safety net in case he suggested going back to her place instead of his.

'Sure. I'll see you there around 8:30,' Bern replied.

Jill sipped her whiskey and waited. She brushed off all the drunk attempts from the guys in the bar as they approached her one at a time. She shot down pick-up line after pick-up line. Jill hated bars.

"Do you need anything else?" the bartender asked.

"No. I'm just waiting for someone," she replied.

Jill sat and waited and watched until she finally saw Bern walk through the doors. It was about 8:20.

"Hey, Alice!" he said, as he gave her a big hug.

"Hey! It's really good to see you!" she said, sliding her hands down his chest after the hug. Jill was going to dive right in head first. He wasn't getting away this time.

"You too! You look amazing!" He politely complimented her.

"What can I get for you, buddy?" the bartender asked.

"A whiskey on the rocks," Bern responded.

"Good choice," Alice said, raising her glass and winking at Bern.

"I'm going to run to the bathroom quick, if you'll excuse me," Bern said.

"I'll be here," Alice replied, as the bartender set Bern's drink down.

Perfect! the blonde bombshell, Alice, thought to herself.

As soon as she saw Bern go into the bathroom, she opened her purse. The 'red panties' were now individually bagged and had been crushed into a fine powder from their previous pill form.

Making sure the bartender was distracted by another patron, Alice dumped the powder into Bern's fresh drink and then stirred it quickly.

"Sorry about that," Bern said, returning to the barstool next to Alice.

"It's okay! Cheers!" Alice said, lifting her glass toward Bern, prompting him to raise his glass in response. The glasses quietly clinked together.

Being a heavy whiskey drinker, Bern took such a large mouthful of the drink that he nearly emptied half of the short glass.

Jill watched in fear as Bern's face contorted a little.

"Wow! That was weird tasting! Almost soapy," he said, examining the drink.

Jill sat mortified. *Distract him!* she told herself.

"He may have put lemon in it because that's how I ordered mine," she said, offering a quick, albeit poor, explanation.

A distraction, not an explanation! she reminded herself silently.

"I do really love your tattoos!" Jill said, running her fingers down Bern's inked arm.

You can do better! she silently encouraged herself.

"Do you want to see my favorite tattoo?" Jill asked.

"Sure! Didn't I see them all at the pool the other night?" Bern asked as he pictured the hot, voluptuous blonde named Alice, in the skimpy red bikini.

"Not this one. I have secret a one," she replied with a sexy grin.

Jill lifted her shirt a little and unbuttoned her skirt. She pulled the front down, exposing her lacy white panties. She slid the sexy underwear down a few inches, showing Bern a tattoo that was on the edge of her right hip — a spot that had been barely covered the other night by her sensuously revealing bikini.

The tattoo was a beautiful series of small stars scattered through a light cosmic dust. They appeared to form a nondescript constellation that swirled around her beautifully smooth skin.

A perfect distraction.

"I have always loved stars," Jill said. "One of my favorite sayings is 'I don't want to count money; I want to count stars'."

Bern raised his drink again, completely forgetting about the odd taste, then stopped before he took a drink.

"Can I get another drink? This time a different whiskey; that one was a little too soapy tasting for me," he told the bartender.

"Sure thing! Sorry about that. Anything for you?" the bartender asked Jill.

"I'm good for now. Everything is perfect, thanks," she replied with a fake smile.

She looked angrily at the tainted drink, that Bern had set aside.

"What do you think about God?" Bern asked, turning to Alice. The question came out of the blue and caught her completely off guard.

This was a question that Bern always asked women whom he thought he saw the potential of being in a serious relationship with. He felt like their answer to that one question gave him an insight into who they really were inside.

"Well...I was raised in a religious home. My dad was the pastor of a church where we lived...ummmm..."

"What's your last name, Alice?" Bern asked, ending her long, awkward pause.

Jill froze.

"Parker..." she said with an odd hesitation, remembering the last name from the Bonnie and Clyde documentary.

Jill quickly took a drink of her whiskey.

"Oh, like...Bonnie?" Bern asked.

Jill choked on her stiff drink. It hurt to swallow.

"Like...who?" Jill said, coughing a little as she played dumb.

"You know, Bonnie and Clyde? That Bonnie...her last name was Parker," Bern said factually, remembering the documentary that he had watched just the other night with his friend, Anna.

"Sorry, my drink went down the wrong pipe," Jill said. Still recovering from coughing, she patted her chest. "Yes, just like Bonnie. You caught me off guard; most people don't know that...I'm impressed," Jill said, still completely rattled.

"I just watched a documentary on it. I watch a lot of documentaries," said Bern.

"Oh, I love documentaries." Jill tried to change the subject.

"Alice Parker," Bern said. "I like it."

Her hands trembled slightly. She ordered another drink. She needed one badly.

Bern talked and flirted with the woman he came to know as Alice. She seemed genuine—not like the other women he "dated." He really liked this one.

Alice Parker.

"So, do you want to go back to my place and smoke some weed?" Bern asked.

"Sure! Let's go!" Jill said enthusiastically. She had been sitting in that damn bar long enough. A couple puffs would take the edge off anyway.

"I'm just going to run to the bathroom first and then we can go," Bern said.

'You look fucking sexy tonight,' Jill texted Bern while he was in the bathroom.

"The night will go as planned," she said to herself softly.

The drunk couple caught a cab. They climbed in the backseat together, still laughing at a joke the bartender had told them on their way out the door.

Bern calmed down his drunk hysterics long enough to give the driver his address, and then they started on their way.

They saw the world pass by through intoxicated eyes. They flirted and chatted with a playful, seductive banter as they rode back to Bern's house over by the old train depot. The warehouse part of the city.

Alice knew that she had this under control.

Chapter 11 – One Hell of a Night.

The intoxicated couple finally arrived at Bern's house after a long, flirtatious cab ride.

"Let's have drinks!" the already very intoxicated Bern said, as he started getting out numerous liquor bottles in the kitchen. "Gin?" he asked.

"Sure!" Jill said, as she slowly walked around Bern's beautiful home. She admired the sophisticated décor and all the amazing art. She would love to own one of his paintings...someday.

Bern poured two glasses of gin over ice and then excused himself to his bedroom.

Jill quickly grabbed her purse and got out the last red panty she had left. The white pill with the red dot was already crushed up like the one before it—the one that Bern had avoided in his off-tasting whiskey at the bar.

She quickly poured the powder into Bern's drink and stirred it.

He's probably too intoxicated to even notice the odd taste, Jill thought…and hoped.

Bern came out of his bedroom and found her holding his drink in the kitchen, just as she finished with it.

"Here's your drink," Alice said with a sexy smile.

Bern took a sip of the drink and didn't even react—no sour face, no scrunched eyebrows.

"Let's smoke some weed!" Bern said, getting his much-used cigar box out.

He lit a joint and passed it to Alice. She puffed it and passed it back.

The couple sat on the couch and smoked the joint. They talked and laughed. Bern was charming and intoxicating. Alice found him irresistible.

She finished the joint and climbed on top of Bern. She kissed down the side of his neck. She could feel that he was excited.

"Let's finish our drinks and go to your bed," Alice whispered in his ear.

Bern finished the tainted drink in three gulps, swallowing all the GHB along with the gin.

Alice grabbed Bern's hand and pulled him up from the couch. His mind felt good and fuzzy.

"Take me to your bed," She commanded.

Bern led her to his heavenly, plush, king-sized bed.

Alice playfully climbed up on the bed, followed by Bern.

Bern reached over and put his hand on the back of Alice's head, sensually kissing her soft lips. He slid the other hand under her shirt, feeling her lace bra with his fingers.

Alice moaned loudly.

She got Bern on his back and climbed on top of his solid, muscular frame. She straddled his body with her long, sexy legs, and then pulled his shirt over his head and threw it on the floor behind her.

Alice looked at Bern's irresistible, shirtless chest. "I want you!" she whispered in his ear. Her blonde hair fell in his face. Alice wanted to ride the sexy artist like a cowgirl.

Bern felt good. He felt out of control. Whatever Alice told him to do, he did. She was fucking amazing! Bern was in heaven.

Alice pulled on his leather belt, unbuckling it. The metal buckle clinked as it freed itself from Bern's waist.

She unbuttoned and unzipped his jeans, sliding them down his thighs and off his legs.

Bern quickly got the irresistible fantasy woman out of her clothes, leaving the gloriously naked blonde kneeling in front of him on his plush bed.

Bern flipped Alice over onto her back with his strong arms. He kissed down her neck to her chest, and then continued down her stomach, stopping between her thighs.

Alice was breathing heavily. She was throbbing. She had no idea it would be like this.

Bern licked her bare skin. His tongue sensuously tickled her as her muscles tensed up. Alice grabbed the sheets, clenching the white Egyptian cotton in her tight fists.

Bern knew exactly what he was doing, and he was very good at it.

Bern wasn't sure how it happened; the night had become such a distorted blur, but he found himself with Alice lying on her back on top of his dresser. Bern stood between Alice's legs, holding one of her ankles in each hand.

"Oh my God!" Alice screamed out in ecstasy.

Bern slammed forcefully against Alice's voluptuous body. He hit her body so hard that the dresser lurched forward. Bern lost his balance and fell backwards, pulling Alice with him. Her nearly perfect naked body landed on top of his. They could fix the dresser later...

Alice slid Bern back inside her. She rode Bern wildly while his hands explored her entire exposed body.

She had a hard time stopping, even after three orgasms.

Bern was so good that she just wanted to keep fucking him, but that wasn't why she was here; she still had work to do. She needed to get paid.

Bern had started to lose consciousness anyway. He was getting soft. She had rode him until he came, and then some.

"Maybe I'll come back for more." she whispered in his ear and then gently touched her lips against his.

The blonde bombshell climbed off of the naked, dazed man, leaving him to fall asleep alone.

"When you wake up, you will remember nothing..." Alice said with a smile. Then she snapped her fingers and quietly laughed.

Bern drifted into a deep, drug-induced unconsciousness that would surely erase the entire memory of the night.

Jill was wet and slippery. Sweat glistened on her smooth curves. Tiny drops of passion that had spilled from her pores. She turned on the shower and stepped under the cold flowing water. She rinsed her body off as her mind wandered.

Barely regaining consciousness for a few seconds, Bern opened his eyes once more, just long enough to see a blurry image of a sexy blonde temptress, naked and wet in his steamy shower.

Nearly every man's fantasy.

Chapter 12 – The Morning After.

Jill sat and looked at Bern lying naked on the bed next to her.

That was by far the best sex she'd ever had.

She leaned over and kissed him on his cheek. "Thanks for everything," she whispered to the unconscious man.

Bern was out cold and wouldn't remember anything when he finally woke up. The red panties had done their job. A classic date rape drug—GHB.

Jill looked around the room. It was pretty messed-up already from the blurry night of rough sex.

"Okay, money...where are you?" she said, as she opened drawers and dug through their contents. Jill was still beautifully naked.

The early morning sun illuminated her soft, radiant skin, and she looked amazing. The brilliant rays coming through the windows outlined her slender curves. It was too bad for Bern that he was unconscious.

Jill had recognized Bern's name on James' phone. She knew he was a successful artist and that he would probably have a good amount of cash or a large quantity of drugs, which she could turn into cash, somewhere in his house.

James thought that Jill was trying to find out if Bern knew anything about the government projects, but she already felt that he didn't know anything and looking very hard would be a waste of time. She felt like she knew who Bern was, even if he had no idea who she really was. Also, she didn't really care to dig, that's not really why she was there. James just gave her an alibi and she used it.

Jill just saw Bern as a potential way out of stripping, at least for a few months. James could get back on his medication. He would turn back into the person she loved. It would be her heaven...her high.

Finally, in the top drawer of the side table, she found a rolled-up stack of bills.

"Yes!" Jill said ecstatically.

She unrolled the bills to get an idea of how much money it was. It looked like about fifty $100 bills—way more than Jill had ever hoped for.

Next, she went to the bathroom and looked in the medicine cabinet, searching for any kind of drugs she could take. She grabbed two prescription bottles, a small mirror, and an out-of-place red lipstick.

She took the cap off the lipstick and drew a heart on Bern's bathroom mirror. "Stick heart," She whispered with a smile.

She put the lipstick back, closed the mirrored door, and walked out to the living room, which was surprisingly still pretty neat and clean. Jill knew this needed to change.

She walked to the kitchen where her purse was. She pulled out the bag with the cocaine—aka one white shirt—and then dumped almost all of it into a small sandwich bag that she found on the counter. She zipped the new bag up and set it down by her purse. She sprinkled some powder on the mirror from the bathroom, making it look dusty.

Jill threw the original, near-empty, powder-covered bag down on the coffee table, along with the small, lightly dusted mirror from the bathroom. To top it off, she threw some rolled-up bills on the table next to the planted items.

Back in the kitchen, she started going through cabinets. She found glasses and more bottles of liquor. She poured liquor in glasses and then dumped them into the sink, making the glasses look sticky and used when they sat out and dried. Some glasses she refilled with liquor, only to add water from the sink, making it look like ice had melted and watered them down.

She spilled scotch on the counter and rum on the floor, halfway cleaning it up and leaving the dirty paper towel behind.

She dumped a couple of liquor bottles out into the sink, completely emptying them both. She left one in the kitchen, lying on its side on the counter.

The other bottle she left on the coffee table in the living room next to the empty bag of coke and two watered-down glasses of whiskey.

Jill opened the cigar box that was still sitting on the coffee table. She took three of the joints and then headed back to the bedroom.

Jill looked around the messy bedroom for her clothes. She found her shirt, her bra, and her skirt but gave up on her white lace panties. They were a small price to pay for such a big fix. Jill now had enough money to keep James on his meds and sane for almost a couple of years.

She made sure she had the cash, the joints, and the prescriptions, and then she headed for the front door.

The now dressed, but still panty less, woman known as Alice grabbed her purse from the counter, shoving her plundered goods into it.

"Well, that was one hell of a night," Jill said, as she walked out of Bern's house, accidentally leaving the zippered sandwich bag of coke behind on the kitchen counter.

She walked about ten blocks until she saw a cab. She rode home in silence, reliving the night from memory. It was fucking amazing. The way Bern felt inside of her was irresistibly sensual. The memory gave Jill chills.

Jill got out her phone and deleted all the messages from 'Bern–the artist' as a precaution. She then went into the phone's menu and wiped all the data, resetting it completely.

It's too bad that Bern won't be able to relive this memory, she thought. She watched the many different people out the car window as the cab passed them by.

Jill made sure the driver wasn't paying attention. He had music on and was focused on the road in front of him. As they drove over one of the city's bridges, Jill rolled her window down. She smelled the stale city air as she breathed in deeply.

After one more check that the driver was still not paying attention to her, Jill took the cell phone—the prepaid phone she used to talk to Bern—and threw it out the car window. The phone tumbled down to the water below. The cab moved too quickly for her to hear the splash, but she still imagined it and the way it sounded.

Jill imagined her alter ego, Alice, standing on the edge of the bridge. She was fed up with the lies. She was fed up with the humiliation and disgrace.

Without a second thought, Alice jumped off the bridge.

Jill imagined Alice plunging into the swift current below, some of her bones breaking on impact. Her lungs burned as they filled with water. She coughed, only causing more water to rush into her body as she choked and spat. Alice's broken limbs could not keep her above water.

The current spun her into a disoriented state that only worsened as the oxygen to her brain started running out. She felt confused, sleepy, and then…nothing.

Jill imagined that Alice died in the river that night. Jill had gotten what she wanted, and she didn't need Alice around anymore. Things were going to get better.

Jill had the driver stop at the pharmacy, where she paid for two more months of James' prescriptions. This left plenty of cash for her to save for the coming months. She also bought one bottle of dark-brown hair dye, the hue that was closest to her natural color.

She knew that she wasn't going to need to keep the blonde for much longer.

Jill silently smiled the rest of the cab ride home.

Chapter 13 – Unimpressed.

Jill got home from Bern's house early Thursday morning. Luckily, James was nowhere to be found, as usual.

Jill got in the shower and washed the smell of hours of amazing sex off of her body, and then she climbed into bed, alone, and quickly fell asleep.

James was probably out following people or doing some more rogue investigating. Jill didn't understand his obsession with the government's mind projects. It's true that she went along with it, as an activist of sorts, but she only did it for him.

Jill hoped this would all change with the medication. Hopefully, James' whole obsession with government mind-control projects would lessen as his brain returned to normal.

Jill awoke to the sound of James coming home in the early afternoon.

"Hey! So how did last night go?" he asked, sitting down softly on the bed next to her.

"I didn't find anything. He doesn't know anything. He's just a normal guy…an artist—not even a scientist," Jill said sleepily.

James' mood suddenly changed; he seemed angered. His eyebrows dropped.

"How good did you look?" he asked inquisitively.

"I looked through everything. I asked questions. There was nothing to find!" Jill explained, needlessly defending herself.

"Tell me about it. What happened?" James asked with a piercing glare.

"Well, we met up at a bar. I slipped him some GHB. Then we went back to his house, where I slipped him more GHB. He was unconscious for hours while I went through his house. He isn't going to remember a thing today. I made the house look like there was a party so he wouldn't notice the mess I left behind. James, he doesn't know anything." Jill tried to assure the doubtful control freak.

"Are you sure?! Why would we have been given his name if he has no information?" James continued to insinuate that Jill hadn't done a good enough job.

"I don't know! Why don't you ask your mysterious contact?" Jill replied bitterly.

"I should have just broken into his place myself..." James said, as he became more agitated.

"I really went through everything! He was drugged and would have told me if he knew anything at all," Jill said.

Jill wasn't lying; she hadn't come across any documents or anything related to government brain scans while she'd been looking for money, which had been her motive.

"Fuck! I knew I should have done it myself. He had to know about or have something," James said, as he rubbed his head. He had an excruciating migraine.

"Well, I'm sorry I didn't find anything. I really think he has nothing to do with it. Maybe we will find something tonight," Jill added, trying to get James off the topic.

"Yeah, at least I'll be there to look myself. I know I'm not going to fuck it up," James said, as he got up and walked to the bathroom.

Jill loathed the condescending James. He always made her feel like she wasn't good enough.

"Have you been taking your prescriptions?" Jill asked cautiously.

"Yes, Jill, I have," James said, rubbing his nose and sniffing from the line of cocaine that he had just snorted. He had purchased a small amount with some money he had taken from Jill's purse. She didn't know.

"Can you try taking just your prescriptions and no street drugs along with them?" Jill said, knowing that pushing the topic was like skating on very thin ice. "Just your prescriptions?"

"Fuck you, Jill! You don't know what my head is like. I take what I need when I need it!" James said defensively, as if Jill was trying to provoke him.

"I'm just saying, so we know if the prescriptions are working. They cost a lot, and I worked really hard to get them for you. If they don't help by themselves, I need to know," Jill said firmly.

"Well, I'm just saying, I know what the fuck I'm doing, Jill!" James snapped back.

Jill knew not to push the subject any further.

"Okay, babe," Jill replied defeated.

"I'm going to relax and get some sleep before tonight," James said, as he crawled into their bed.

"I'm getting up; I have some errands to run. I'll see you when I get back," Jill said, as she went to the bathroom and turned on the shower.

She stood in the shower as the warm water rushed down her bare skin. The liquid warmth calmed her down as she took a deep breath.

James was asleep by the time Jill got out and dried off.

She got dressed and headed down to the library, stopping for a quick hotdog from a street vendor along the way.

Jill didn't have errands to run, but she knew James was on edge, and she didn't want any problems, especially today, with tonight's plan just hours away.

In the library, Jill found a comfortable seat and a book of classic poetry. She needed to get her mind away from her own thoughts. Her eyes pored quickly over words on pages, ink on fibers. The first poem that she read, made her stop to think.

I am not yours, not lost in you,
Not lost, although I long to be
Lost as a candle lit at noon,
Lost as a snowflake in the sea.

You love me, and I find you still
A spirit beautiful and bright,
Yet I am I, who long to be
Lost as a light is lost in light.

Oh plunge me deep in love— put out
My senses, leave me deaf and blind,
Swept by the tempest of your love,
A taper in a rushing wind.

-Sara Teasdale

Jill continued to read, clearing her mind of anything negative.

She was trying to forget about the upcoming night and the task at hand.

Jill and James hadn't really discussed tonight's plan much. She still didn't really know what to expect; but again, that was part of the excitement—the adrenaline.

Jill wasn't sure if she hoped they would find something or that they wouldn't find anything.

Finding something would just take them further down into James' conspiracy rabbit hole. Not finding something meant that James might get his mind set on trying to go to Boston again.

Jill was torn.

Either way, she just needed to clear her mind. She read for a few hours, losing herself in a sea of beautiful words—a false reality on paper that satisfyingly became her own. For a short time, she became those characters about whom she read.

Jill checked the time on her phone and saw that James had sent a picture. It was a screenshot of a message that he had gotten. It was from a phone number that she didn't recognize.

"Breaking in to his apartment then won't be a problem. He will be away sailing. No one will be there."

The screenshot of the message read.

James followed the picture up with a message of his own.

"The person I got the info from sent this message to me. No one is even going to be there. No one is home. It's going to be fine."

This was his attempt to put her at ease. He wanted her to feel like there was nothing to worry about. The last thing he needed was her to be a troublesome liability.

Jill deleted the picture and threw her phone aside. It didn't really make her feel any better. She pushed the thoughts of tonight back out of her mind. There were only had a few pages left of one of her favorite books. She finished the story and smiled. The ending was as good as she remembered. She gathered up her thing, then she headed home.

It was a beautiful evening. As she walked along, she listened to the city. It sounded unusually calm. It was a welcomed change.

As Jill thought about the night's plan, she reassured herself that it wasn't a big deal. She had broken into houses before. Being a junky takes you through some really tough times that most people never have to experience. Maybe Jill would find some money or valuables to hide from James. She always looked on the bright side of things.

Jill hoped more than anything that they wouldn't run into any problems tonight.

Chapter 14 – Guns.

Okay, so here is how tonight is going to go. We need to stick with the plan," James explained. "We have two guns but only bullets for one of them."

"Guns?!" Jill asked, surprised. "You said he wasn't going to be home! That picture of the message you sent, said he was going to be away sailing."

"Yeah, we shouldn't need them, but just in case," James assured her.

"I don't really want to take a gun," Jill said, shaking her head.

"Perfect, you can take the empty one. It's a .38. I don't have bullets that size anyway. I do have .9mm bullets, so I'll take that one."

"Okay..." Jill hesitantly agreed, since the gun wasn't going to be loaded; that and the fact that, with James in control, she really didn't have a choice.

"I found these ski masks. We should wear them in case anyone sees us. And these..." James handed Jill a long, old-looking aluminum flashlight, keeping a second one for himself.

This was turning into something a little more serious than Jill had imagined.

Sure, she used to break into houses—slip a credit card through the latch. Sneak in through the back door, maybe a window. Take a few things and leave. But it was never this serious.

"James...maybe we shouldn't do this. I mean, what if this guy doesn't even know anything? This is a pretty big risk," she said, showing signs of her worry about a plan that seemed to be progressing from petty breaking and entering to potential felony armed robbery and maybe even assault.

She knew this could completely ruin the life she had been trying to build for them.

"We are just going to go in and look for the documents. It's not going to be a big deal," James calmly reassured her. "He probably won't even know we were ever there."

"Well, what is the plan anyway?" Jill inquired, never having heard any solid details.

"Apparently this guy has classified documents about some mind experiments the government did. Rumor has it, he may have even been one of the doctors that tested creating fake memories."

"Oh. Wow."

"We are going to go over there after it gets dark but early enough that the city is still really noisy. We will just go in and look for documents, starting with obvious places first like desks, filing cabinets, and drawers. Then, once we have gone through everything, we will leave. It won't be a big deal. He won't even be there. I want to be in and out in less than an hour. That's the plan," James explained calmly.

His explanation probably shouldn't have been good enough to calm Jill, but it was and it did.

"Okay...well...I'm going to take a shower," Jill said, as she pulled her shirt over her head and walked into the bathroom.

She didn't need another shower; she had just taken one a few hours earlier. But Jill wanted to just relax in the soothing, warm water again. She didn't want to worry about needing to carry a gun or how bad James was at actually planning things.

The warm water from the shower felt good on Jill's naked body. She watched the crystal clear droplets bounce off her soft skin. She felt calm.

She heard a few soft bangs on the other side of the wall, but she ignored them and finished her shower.

The soap suds collected beautifully on her naked skin. Little white bubbles rode streams of water that flowed down her body, like little seductive waterfalls flowing over the most beautiful terrain ever seen.

Jill didn't feel like shaving. With the money from Bern she didn't have to strip anymore and not stripping meant that Jill could skip shaving for a few days if she wanted. As odd as it may sound, this one small detail made her feel like she was free again.

Jill got out and dried her hair with a towel. She looked at the shoulder-length blonde strands in the mirror. She didn't like her hair and couldn't wait until it was back to brown.

She dried her body off, looking at her glorious nude reflection in the mirror.

"Jill!" James yelled. "Jill...what the fuck?!" he yelled more loudly.

Jill opened the door and saw James standing in front of her. His face was red, and his eyebrows were low.

"I found this cash you were hiding from me. You fucking bitch! How much money have you been hiding from me?!" James stood in front of her with a rolled-up stack of bills in his hand. He grabbed Jill's left wrist and twisted it. A sharp pain shot up to her elbow. Her towel fell to the floor. Jill stood naked, exposed, vulnerable and at the complete mercy of James. Jill closed her hazel eyes tightly and clenched her teeth.

James waved the stack of one-hundred-dollar bills in her face—about sixty-five of them, if she remembered correctly. That was everything. It was the money from Bern plus what was left from stripping.

"Don't you EVER keep things from me!" James screamed.

He squeezed and twisted Jill's wrist harder. The pain was excruciating and made her legs want to buckle. She was sure her bones were going to snap at any second

James took the stack of money, shoved it into the pocket of his ripped jeans, and then he let go of Jill's wrist.

James had taken everything.

"Ouch!" Jill said quietly with a pained expression on her face as she rubbed her arm. Her eyes watered as she tried not to show her tears.

"Okay, let's go do this," James commanded, pointing to the ski masks, guns, and flashlights.

Jill reluctantly picked the items up and put them in a fabric bag she used for groceries. She got dressed in dark, comfortable clothes and running shoes.

The couple caught a cab and headed over to an area near the address that James had been given.

As they rode silently in the cab, Jill had the worst feeling in the pit of her stomach—a feeling that let her know that this was a very bad idea. She was so worried about the night that she had no time to really process that James had just taken all the money she had worked hard for—all the money she earned for him, for his medication, to treat his debilitating and violent mental illness. Prescriptions to calm the demons.

They stopped at an intersection, and James paid the cab driver with Jill's money.

"Okay, it's a just few blocks this way," he said, pointing as they got out of the cab.

Under the cloak of darkness, the dangerous couple headed on their way.

As they walked down the street, Jill toted the two handguns in a bag over her shoulder. She thought about how James let her carry both guns on purpose. You could get ten years just for having a gun during a crime; he let her take that risk. He wasn't stupid.

As they approached the building, Jill quietly turned to James and said, "This doesn't look like a place a successful scientist would live. Are you sure you have the right address?"

"Yes, this is the address. I'm positive," James said. "Shhhhhhhhh...now."

They got to the front entrance of the lobby. The security keypad lock was broken. They didn't even need to enter a code; the lock just opened. They quietly walked up the stairs to the third floor.

They stood in front of the dark-brown wooden door. It looked so old. Jill could see the fine grain and the years of wear. It was a beautiful door.

James tapped Jill's shoulder and pointed to the bag. She handed him a ski mask, a flashlight, and a loaded gun.

The couple put on the black wool masks that only showed their eyes.

James gave Jill a quick thumbs-up.

Jill's stomach sank.

For the first time ever, she wished she was stripping.

Chapter 15 – An Accident.

Jill stood nervously as James pried the lock open. The black mask on her face was hot and scratchy. It made her cheeks itch.

James popped the lock open and walked in; as usual, Jill followed.

The couple froze, like deer in the headlights, at the sight of the startled, gray-haired older gentleman standing across the room.

In a split second, the two masked villains instinctively had their guns pointed at the man. He had his hands up in front of him, showing no resistance.

"Where are the documents?" James barked.

"What documents?" the old man, questioned in a confused, trembling voice.

Jill's hands shook. The unloaded weapon felt like it weighed a hundred pounds now.

"Any of the documents about the mind testing and memory engineering! The truth about what the tests were for. Just give us those and we will leave. We don't want to hurt you," James said firmly, without any hint of sympathy.

"I don't have much; all that was confidential. We didn't really keep anything from that, but I'll give you everything I have." The old man cautiously walked to a nearby desk.

James watched the man slowly reach down and open a drawer.

Within a split second, James was looking down the dark, black barrel of a semi-automatic handgun.

CLICK!

Time slowed down as the gun took aim on Jill next. She froze as she saw light reflect off the chrome trim along the grip.

CLICK!

A second attempt, aimed at Jill's head; it would have been fatal.

BANG!

James felt the pressure of the trigger under his finger as his gun recoiled. The old man had already pulled the gun and attempted to shoot twice before James had even fired. The gray-haired defender's reaction had been surprisingly quick, like a snake striking.

James' bullet hit the old, innocent man directly in the middle of his chest with an impact that was brutal. Crimson blood sprayed out of the bullet hole almost immediately.

The perfect couple watched the old man stumble backwards, tripping over an office chair. He spun around and fell to the floor, dropping his unloaded gun. He grabbed his chest and gasped.

James, holding the now smoking gun, looked into the man's eyes as he lay alone on the floor, dying.

Jill tried to ignore the sound of the gentle old man's lungs gurgling. She tried not to hear his labored breathing or his gasps. She closed her beautiful, hazel eyes as the blood started to pool on the wooden floorboards surrounding him.

"We are lucky his gun didn't fire; he would have killed us both. Goddamn it, he was fast! He must have had some kind of special training."

"We almost died," Jill said with closed eyes.

"Yep."

"You killed him."

"Yeah; he's gone. Help me look around," James said nonchalantly.

"Shouldn't we get the hell out of here?! I mean, you just shot a retired scientist and killed him! He wasn't even supposed to be here! This isn't just a robbery anymore; it's murder! Things just changed in a big way!" The stunned woman quickly became very anxious.

Jill felt horrible. The poor old man didn't deserve this. Why was he even here? Why was *she* even here?! What happened to sailing? This wasn't supposed to happen! She just wanted to leave, forget about the documents and the stupid fucking project, and get high...alone.

"What about the gunshot? The cops are going to come!" she said, as she started to become more frantic.

"Look, calm down. It doesn't really matter! No one is coming because of that gunshot. People hear gunshots all the time on this side of the city, and even if someone did call, we still have a good thirty minutes before anyone gets here."

Jill reluctantly started looking through the dead man's personal belongings.

James abruptly broke the silence.

"I knew he wasn't going sailing until next week. I just didn't want to wait, so I said he would be gone this week. Don't be mad. You wouldn't have come this week if I hadn't lied about it. It was just some old guy. I didn't think confronting him would be a problem. I definitely didn't think he'd pull a gun out like a trained mercenary. Either way, I'm sure we're going to find something worthwhile," James said, clearly showing what a horrible person he really was inside.

Jill was shocked. She didn't believe that James was actually cold-blooded and heartless…until he proved it at that very moment. She thought back to the picture, of the message, that he sent to put her at ease.

"Breaking in then won't be a problem. He will be away sailing. No one will be there."

Little did she know, James had intentionally deleted the previous message. The message which clarified that the sailing trip wasn't this week.

"He lives alone. Next week is when he will be out of town. It would be best to wait until the middle of next week."

All she knew now, though, was that she just had to stay as calm as possible to make it through this.

"Don't you feel bad at all about going through all his stuff?" Jill asked, shaking her head.

"No. He's dead. He doesn't care anymore," James said with a laugh, as if he thought Jill's question was completely absurd.

James was already going through some papers from a filing cabinet. Jill walked to the closed blinds and opened them up. The little bit of extra illumination from the city's night lights made the apartment feel less gloomy and sad.

Jill looked at the family pictures on the bookcase. She looked at the happy man in them—the man who now lay dead on the floor because of her.

She looked closely at a beautiful metal antique box.

The box had an intricate pattern engraved on all sides and a small, cast-iron lock on the front. She ran her finger along the edge of the box.

Jill read the faint words on the lock: 'Omnis cognitionis intra.'

"You should take that!" James suggested, as he watched her admiring it.

"No way! I'm not taking anything from this man. I don't deserve anything, especially this beautiful box. He wasn't supposed to be here. I would have broken in and taken the box, sure, but we took his life! It's not right to take anything else." Jill stood firm with her conscience. "Take the records and whatever you want, but not me. I can't!" she continued.

"Are you serious? I'll take the fucking box myself!" James said angrily, storming over and grabbing the metal box from the bookshelf. He examined it closely, admiring the intricate design. "I bet it's worth some money." He set the antique box down by the front door so he wouldn't forget it on their way out. "Now, help me go through some fucking papers, instead of browsing through the stuff you aren't going to steal!"

Jill gazed over at the beautiful box sitting by the front door and sighed. She stood next to James, unwillingly looking for documents and medical records. She just wanted to get the hell out of there; the faster they got through the place, the sooner she could leave. At this point, leaving was her only motivation for helping at all.

On occasion, she would catch a glimpse of David's body, she would cringe, and her eyes would water. She had to fight back the tears because of James. Of all the bad things Jill had done throughout her life as a junky, this right here was the absolute lowest.

Jill kept checking the clock, getting more antsy as time slowly crawled.

After about twenty-five minutes, they had some small stacks of what James thought were very interesting papers and reports. There were brain scans and test files about memory engineering and artificial memory fabrication. James was amazed at all the evidence they had found.

This was James' heaven.

"We've got to get out of here soon," he said, looking at the clock on the wall. "I've got to piss first though." He quickly walked into the bathroom.

Jill looked over at the beautiful metal antique box still sitting by the front door.

She couldn't let him take it; it just wasn't right. She hurried over and picked it up, ushering it swiftly back to its original home on the bookcase, right between two framed pictures of the old man and who must have been his happy, beautiful wife.

Passing back by David's body, Jill heard faint gurgling. He wasn't dead yet! She picked up a towel and used it to grab David's house phone. She dialed 911 and quickly put the phone inside the towel, muffling any sounds from inside the apartment.

Jill quickly got back to the spot she'd been in when James had left for the bathroom. She pretended to be finishing up with the last stack of papers, straightening them neatly, as if she were playing a secretarial role. Pretending was, luckily, one of the few things she was good at.

"Okay, we're done. We can go now," she said, as James walked out of the bathroom.

"Let's get the hell out of here!" James ordered, always making sure he was the one in charge.

They each grabbed a stack of papers of about 500 sheets. The rest they left scattered across the retired scientist's apartment.

"Okay, we aren't forgetting anything, are we?" he asked, looking back at Jill.

Jill looked over at the now empty spot by the front door where the antique box had been.

"Nope...nothing," she said, as she slowly shook her head.

"Alright! Let's go!" James said with the satisfied arrogance of a big-game hunter after a large, elusive kill.

Walking out the front door behind James, Jill grabbed the towel that had David's house phone in it. The phone fell to the floor, and she threw the towel down.

The two left the apartment, shedding their black clothes on the way. They hit the dark street looking like any other couple—James, a handsomely chiseled blonde man with a perfectly built frame, and Jill, a beautiful, sexy blonde with the body of stripper.

In the apartment just above them on the third floor lay an innocent, retired scientist who was now considered dead.

The couple walked about two miles before they caught a cab. The, almost thirty blocks seemed to take forever, especially for Jill, who carried the same bag with the guns, flashlights, and masks as before, but now with the added weight of about one thousand sheets of paper.

"So, I think we really found some amazing things! This could blow the government's whole mind-control projects right out into the open!" James said with sincere enthusiasm.

"Mmmhhhmm…" Jill muttered, not paying attention to his rambling about all the things she didn't give a damn about.

The sound of James' voice now made her feel physically ill. He had just taken the life of an innocent man and seemed completely unfazed. Even joyous. Maybe the scientist was a father, a grandfather, a husband. James' stupid conspiracy theory was apparently more important than this man's life, and Jill could not comprehend that.

The rest of the walk was near silent. Jill trailed about ten feet behind James, trying to look at him as little as possible.

The cab ride home was also mostly silent.

At one point, James said, "My heart is pounding! Feel it!" He grabbed Jill's hand and put it against his chest. She pulled it away as fast as she could, disgusted by his continued enthusiasm for the night's events.

They arrived at an intersection about five blocks from their apartment, and then they walked the rest of the way home. Jill still trailed about ten feet behind. The couple remained silent the entire time.

Jill looked up at the stars as she walked. The few that she could see past the bright lights of the city twinkled beautifully.

Chapter 16 – The Nightmares.

Jill quickly walked into their apartment first and headed straight for the shower.

She stood under the hot water, trying to forget the night. She could still see the older man's kind face every time she closed her eyes. She could still hear him gasping for air and smell the unmistakable scent of gunpowder. Nothing she could do was going to erase the night's events.

"Wow! That was fucking crazy, huh?" James said, as he walked into the bathroom. "My heart is still pounding!" He held his hand to his chest as the palpitating muscle made his hand move with every beat. He felt alive.

Jill didn't reply. She covered her ears with her hands and put her face directly into the shower's stream of hot water.

James walked out of the bathroom. Jill heard him rummaging around, and then she heard the front door close.

Jill was glad. She didn't want to even look at him right now. She still couldn't believe that he had lied about the man being out of town sailing. She had believed a lie that cost an innocent person his life.

After her shower, Jill solemnly slid into a cozy pair of old, worn-out pajamas, and then quietly slipped into bed.

She tossed and turned; she covered her head with a pillow. No matter what she did, she still heard the gunshot, and she still saw the blood. She remembered the way David's eyes looked at her as he gasped, confused and in shock. She could still see his pain, as she unwillingly relived the night over and over.

Jill finally fell asleep after a couple of exhausting hours of tormenting insomnia. Unfortunately, sleep didn't last long.

Startled by a noise, she awoke suddenly to a fuzzy vision of an older man standing over her.

Jill was still lying in bed. She clenched the sheets tightly in her hands.

The man put his hand over her mouth and a large, black handgun to her head.

"Shhhhhhhhhh," he whispered.

Jill closed her eyes and lay there for what seemed like an eternity. She could feel the pressure of the leather-gloved hand on her jaw. She could feel the cold steel barrel pressing against her forehead.

BANG!

Jill sat straight up in bed, wide-eyed and sweaty. Her heart was pounding.

"Fuck!" she yelled.

The sound of James slamming the front door as he returned home abruptly woke her from the nightmare. Jill covered her face with her hands. They were trembling slightly. She was alone in her dark room. The nightmare had felt so horribly real.

She could hear James in the kitchen. She hoped that he stayed out of the shadowy bedroom, which she had turned into a remorseful sanctuary.

Jill, in her restlessness, had gotten up earlier to shut the door and close all the blinds and curtains.

She lay in the darkness, listening to James' movements. It sounded like he was making something to eat in their small kitchen. Then, she heard him turn on the TV and sit down on the couch. She heard the familiar sound of the springs squeak under his weight.

Lying in their small bed alone in the dark, Jill could hear a baseball game.

The sound of a baseball game in the background was always relaxing to her. Her dad and brother used to listen to baseball games on the radio all the time when she was little.

The soothing sound of the game reminded her of her older brother, who had loved the sport as a kid. Jill missed him dearly.

Jill's father didn't abuse her brother the same way he did Jill and her mother; but, unfortunately, he did push him very hard to succeed.

Jill remembered the day they lost her brother. She remembered seeing him on his bike and seeing the oncoming car. She remembered screaming out loud as she watched her brother's twisted body hit the windshield and fall to the pavement. She remembered the way it sounded—body smashing into glass, crystal shards showering the cement. The car tires didn't screech to a stop until it was too late.

Their mother, who had run into the street almost immediately, fell to her knees and held the dying boy in her arms. Jill saw death up close for the first time that day.

Jill was about ten years old back then. This was when her family really spiraled out of control and fell apart. This was when her dad became much more abusive and her mother became deeply depressed. Her brother had helped protect Jill from their father; but at the vulnerable age of ten, that protection was suddenly gone.

That was a memory she would never forget—the memory of her brother dying. Now this was the second time she had seen death up close; watching David die...because of her...was a new memory that she would never be able to forget.

Jill stayed in the dark bedroom of the small apartment for the rest of the day, like a child hiding from monsters. But instead of something imaginary in the closet or under the bed, Jill hid in the dark from a real monster, named James.

She finally drifted off to sleep to the faint sounds of a baseball game and the fond memories of her brother, whom she still missed terribly. She didn't stir again until she heard a loud thud that sounded like a body hitting the floor.

Jill opened her hazel eyes and found herself standing in David's apartment again. The older man pulled his hand out of the desk drawer with lightning speed.

BANG!

Jill quickly looked over at James as the first shot hit him right in the neck. Blood sprayed out of the fleshy bullet hole, in his throat, as his head slumped forward.

The stunned Jill turned back and looked down the barrel of the smoking gun. Time slowed down.

BANG!

Jill saw a bright flash and felt an excruciating, hot pressure on her chest, followed by a sharp, intense, stabbing pain.

She fell to the floor, gasping for air. Her lungs gurgled with blood. They burned like fire. The pain was excruciating.

She looked over at James, who was choking and coughing as blood spilled violently from his neck.

The man walked over to Jill. She tried to scream but couldn't.

She looked at the face behind the gun. It was still kind and old. The eyes that lined the sight up on her head gazed lovingly at the target. A man who would normally never hurt anyone had turned into a swift, deadly assassin.

"Hey!" a loud voice said.

Jill's eyes flew wide open, awakened from another nightmare by James' voice and a gentle nudge.

"Oh my God! I just had...the worst...nightmare!" Jill said, trying to slow down her rapid breathing.

"Do we have any drugs?" James asked. His hands were shaking.

"There is valium and I think a couple morphine in the bottle on the bathroom counter," Jill said, covering her eyes.

James got up and went to the bathroom, shutting the bedroom door behind him.

Jill put her pillow back over her head. She was ready to take some drugs too, if it meant she could get some sleep without the nightmares. Jill wanted nothing more than to escape the nightmares. But before she even had time to contemplate getting up, the completely exhausted vixen fell asleep once again.

Chapter 17 – A Personal Attack.

Jill woke up to the sound of the toilet flushing three times in a row, the banging of the toilet seat, and the splashing of water.

"What the fuck?!" she said, as she jumped out of bed and ran to their small bathroom, wearing only a pair of blue lace underwear and an old white tank top. In her search for some peaceful rest, Jill had shed the pajamas that she had previously been wearing.

The toilet was starting to overflow. Water started pooling everywhere. Lying on the floor, almost floating now in the collecting water, Jill saw three empty prescription bottles.

James had thrown all his expensive, prescription drugs into the toilet, then tried to flush them away.

"What the fuck?!" she screamed again, throwing her hands in the air.

She was exhausted, and her nerves were shot. She couldn't fucking take this anymore. She threw a couple towels down on the floor to collect the water.

"James, you need help! If you don't take your medication, I can't be with you anymore. I can't do this!" Jill yelled at him as angry tears fell.

"You want me to take drugs that make me someone else!" James screamed. In a blind fury, he lunged at Jill, his fist landing a harsh blow to the side of her beautiful, delicate face.

Jill stumbled backwards out of the bathroom and into the living room. She covered her face for protection as James thrust his hands into her chest, pushing her back further. As she started to lose her balance, her calves hit the coffee table, sending her falling back-first through the glass tabletop.

The sound of the glass shattering was deafening. Crystal shards showered down on the worn, wooden floor. Jill felt the sting of the cuts on the backs of her arms almost instantly.

The glass coffee table was one of the few things the couple had bought together. A simple piece of furniture. It symbolized progress—an attempt to move forward with a normal, stable life together. Now it symbolically lay shattered underneath Jill's bleeding, bruised body.

She screamed out in pain as blood started dripping from the small cuts on her skin.

"Fuck you, Jill! You don't control me!" James had stopped coming toward her. With clenched fists, he now stood towering in front of her fallen, damaged figure. He was breathing heavily, and his face was red.

"Fuck you! Just leave me alone!" Jill cried out, covering her face from the additional blows that she had learned to expect over the years. The small trails of blood had trickled down Jill's arms onto her fingers and palms. That blood was now smeared across her tear-soaked face.

James turned, grabbed the apartment keys off the counter, and then walked out through the front door, slamming it behind him.

Jill didn't uncover her face or open her eyes until she heard James out on the street below, still cursing and yelling, oblivious to strangers' awkward stares.

She pulled herself up and stumbled to the bathroom, leaving small drops of what looked like crimson velvet on the old wooden floorboards behind her.

Jill grabbed a white towel and wiped her arms, leaving bright red streaks on the cheap, scratchy terry cloth fabric.

She looked closely at her face in the mirror. Her lip was already starting to swell, and she was sure the side of her face would be bruised from James' fist.

"I can't do this anymore," she said to herself, as she leaned with her back against the wall.

The cuts on her arms looked like minor scratches once they were cleaned up. Given the amount of blood, Jill expected cuts that were far worse than what she was now looking at.

She opened the medicine cabinet and got out a bottle of aspirin. She struggled to get the bottle open, clawing at the top and smacking the bottle violently down on the counter.

"Fuuuuuck!" she yelled, as she threw the unopened bottle at her reflection in the mirror. It bounced off and disappeared into the clutter of the messy bathroom.

Jill slid down the wall, not stopping until she was sitting on the floor. She put her head in her hands and cried.

"How did this happen?" she whispered softly, between sobs.

Kitty came running up from his hiding spot behind the couch, as soon as he felt like it was safe. He gently touched one of Jill's finger with his nose as if to check on her. He licked the back of her hand with his rough tongue, then he stretched out in front of her and closed his eyes.

Jill slowly pet his fur and thought about how she and James should leave town for a while. They'd just shot a man; it seemed like the next logical step.

"Damn it," she sobbed.

Shooting David had sealed Jill's fate with James. She didn't feel like she could leave him now. He probably wouldn't let her leave anyway—not with her knowing that he was the killer…not with her being a witness. She knew he would be worried that she would rat him out. Unmedicated James trusted no one. Jill felt like there was no way out now. No escape.

Jill cleaned up the rest of her own blood and looked around the bathroom, which was still wet from the from the overflowed toilet.

She picked up the three empty prescription bottles and threw them in the small garbage can. Jill was destroyed and heartbroken as she threw away the bottles that symbolized her only hope for a normal life.

She threw another towel down to soak up the remainder of the water. The toilet had stopped overflowing; it drained and flushed like normal now.

Jill walked out of the bathroom and followed the dripped trail of crimson blood to the scattered pile of sparkling glass shards. The table frame on which the glass had sat was still standing. It had caught Jill's arms on both sides when she'd fallen. She knew that she would probably have bruises from it.

Jill got the broom and dustpan and started sweeping up the broken pieces. She cleaned her blood off the wooden floor and threw everything away.

Hurt and exhausted, Jill sat on the couch. She had to work at the bar tonight and, of course, she didn't want to. At least it would keep her busy and not thinking about everything. She always looked for the positive side of things, no matter how bad they seemed.

Jill turned on the TV and looked for anything mind-numbing to watch. Finding nothing she wanted, she grabbed her favorite book off her nightstand, the special gift from her mother.

Jill read about Alice and what she found on the other side of the mirror—a whole new world.

Jill's mind was suddenly pulled out of the book by the sound of James coming home. She cringed and had the urge to hide somewhere, but unfortunately it was too late.

"Hey, I'm sorry," he said. "Everything is just really hard...you know? I'm going to only take my prescriptions—no street drugs—and see how it goes. I promise," James tried to convince Jill.

"You can be such a dick. That shit hurt! Look at my arms and my face!" she said, crying between sentences.

"I'm sorry. I didn't mean to hurt you, and I didn't want you to fall. I was angry and afraid, so I left." James always played the victim when he felt like he needed to.

"James, I love you! I just want you to be normal. I want our life to be normal!"

"I know. I'm sorry," he replied quietly.

Jill was quick to accept his generic apology, as usual. Of course she forgave him...she always did.

"We need to go to his funeral," James said, awkwardly breaking the long silence.

"I am not going to his funeral...no way!" Jill protested. "James, I can't. I've been having nightmares. I can't do it."

Jill hadn't been to a funeral since she had to look at her young brother lying in a casket when she was ten years old. She knew that she would absolutely break down if she went.

"We could probably find something out there...think about it!" James was usually very persuasive, but not this time. Jill stood firm.

"No way! We should probably do something else anyway. Hey, what about Anna Smith's house? We haven't looked at anything there. We should go there and look while we know she is at the funeral."

Jill thought her idea was brilliant.

"We just need to watch the obituaries in the paper to find out when and where," James noted, proudly showing Jill that he had bought a newspaper earlier.

"Ok, well, you go to the funeral and be a lookout while I go to Anna's house and look through it. You just make sure she's there at the funeral. It will work out perfectly." Jill tried hard to sell James on the plan—anything to get out of going to the gentle old man's funeral…a funeral that she felt responsible for. An event set in motion by James lies.

Jill knew that she couldn't go to that funeral no matter what. The guilt would eat her alive if she did.

"Okay, let's do that then. It will be perfect since we know she won't be home," James agreed.

Jill was relieved to know that she wouldn't have to attend the funeral of the man she had watched dying…the man she hadn't helped or reached out to…the man they had murdered.

On the other hand though, a small part of her optimistic side thought maybe the man had lived. Maybe her phone call had been enough to get him help in time. She thought back to the sounds of him dying, and she pictured the vast amount of blood that pooled on the wooden floor.

Probably not, she sadly thought; there was going to be a funeral.

James found it—a small entry in the obituaries.

"Here it is. This is it." James pointed. "I'll go to the funeral while you go to her house and look for any classified documents or evidence. I will be the lookout and text you when she's leaving." He wanted to be in control of her idea.

Jill was less than excited.

James spent the next few days leading up to the funeral reviewing the documents from David's apartment. He looked at them repeatedly but never really found anything substantial.

He hoped that the funeral and Anna's apartment would pay off big.

Chapter 18 – A Thrift Store Suit.

"I look stupid!" James said, looking at himself in the mirror.

He was wearing a used, odd-fitting dress suit from a thrift store—his intended funeral attire. The suit was a dark gray with a slight shine to it. James wore a button-down white shirt underneath, and on his feet were a black pair of dress shoes that were worn but mostly polished. A jet-black tie choked his neck, and he hated it.

Overall, it was a pretty suave outfit—all from a cheap thrift store in the city.

"No, you look handsome. You will be fine. You will blend right in," Jill said, adjusting James' stiff collar.

"Do we need to go over this again?" he asked, questioning Jill's abilities, as usual.

"No, I got it. I'll be leaving in about thirty minutes." She checked the time on her phone.

This was Jill's way of making sure no one else got hurt. Any other day and this woman, Anna, may be home and may end up getting shot too. Jill couldn't let that happen again, and she knew that James could easily do it again.

The handsome, blonde man got into a car parked out front and drove away. He had borrowed the old, beat-up car from a guy he got high with. James drove to the other side of the city, stopping at a building on the outskirts.

It was a beautiful building—white with orange brick— and two large trees shaded the small front lawn.

James walked into the old funeral home. Inside, it was cold and funny-smelling, like an old church.

He took a seat in the back, blending in perfectly with the other guests—the ones who were truly there mourning.

He could see Anna and Bern sitting together about fifteen rows ahead of him.

The funeral director came to the front of the room.

"Thank you all for coming out tonight. We have a special presentation for you," he said, greeting the audience from the front of the room.

James' cell phone suddenly rang with a loud, disruptive sound that made everyone turn their attention to him. He quickly fumbled through his many pockets as he stood up to leave. He finally found the phone in a pocket inside his used suit jacket. He quickly swiped the screen, answering the horribly timed call and silencing the disruptive ringer.

"Hello..." James answered softly but angrily. He quickly walked toward the door, as the service was just beginning.

The audience was unanimously appalled, however, James could distinguish a couple of familiar voices above the soft, disgusted rumbling.

"Are you kidding me?! Who the hell does that?! What did he come here for? That makes me so mad! Show some respect!" Anna could be heard whispering loudly to Bern, disgusted and angry, as they sat at the front of the room, looking back.

"Ridiculous," Stan said quietly, shaking his head as he sat next to them.

"I guess on that note, I should remind all of you to turn your phones off please." The funeral director's voice could be heard fading into the background.

"What the fuck?!" James said, as he exited the building.

"I just wanted to be sure you were there watching them. I'm getting ready to leave. Did you make it in time?" Jill asked.

"What the fuck did you call me for when you knew it would be starting?!" James asked angrily.

"Wait...you went inside? James! Why the hell did you go inside?!" Jill asked excitedly.

"Because it's a funeral, Jill!" James snapped back.

"I thought you were going to just watch them from outside in the car. We talked about this!" Jill said, defending herself.

"You couldn't have just texted instead of calling?" James responded, arguing like he usually did.

"You couldn't have just watched from outside like we talked about, or silenced your phone like a normal person at a fucking funeral?!" Jill was aggravated at another one of James' off-plan decisions.

"Why did you even go inside?" Jill pushed for any hint of logic.

"Because I wanted to, Jill! Now stop fucking bitching!" James said, as the tension between them quickly escalated.

In frustration, Jill knocked the stack of medical records and random papers she was looking through off of the table and onto the floor.

James looked at his phone. 'Call ended' the screen read.

"Fuck!" he said, as he stood on the sidewalk in front of the funeral home, looking at his phone.

'YOU BETTER FUCKING TEXT ME IF THEY LEAVE!'

A new message from Jill read.

Jill threw her phone in her bag and headed to the bus stop. It was a quick ride to the apartment of a scientist named Anna.

James put his phone away, and peering through the front window, he saw what looked like a film being played inside the funeral home. The lights were so dim now that he could no longer even see the casket at the front of the room.

"What the hell is this?" he said to himself quietly.

Letting his curiosity get the best of him, he quietly walked back into the dimly lit funeral home, from which he had hastily departed. This time, his phone was on silent.

He watched from the back of the room as the pictures changed on the big screen. James was mesmerized by the private screening of one man's personal life—a man named David.

To see the man whom he had killed portrayed so intimately made James actually feel kind of bad for once. He had taken this man's life—a life that, while before just belonged to a stranger, a random old man, had now become that of a real person. A person who's life story was being told in front of him. Little did the audience know that the man, who put an end to the story, was standing right behind them. A shadow in the back of the room.

The woman projected on the screen continued talking as James stood in the back of the old, funny-smelling funeral home and hung on every word.

"All of you are here today because you shared our life with us in one way or another, and we wanted to thank you for that. We are grateful to have known every one of you. We hope you are all still smiling and that you all keep smiling."

The movie continued, and James started to see the life he had taken much differently.

He watched in wonder as he heard the dead man speak at the end. David addressed the audience with gratitude that they were there to share this evening with him and his wife.

No one had any idea that they were all there tonight because of the handsome, blonde man who was watching the same intimate 'thank you' as they were. The man in the thrift store suit.

After the funeral, James sat in the borrowed car—a beat-up, 1978, four-door station wagon—and watched for Anna to leave the funeral.

He saw Bern and Anna talking as they slowly walked to Bern's black Porsche.

'They are leaving now!' James sent the warning text message to Jill.

Back at Anna's apartment, Jill had been going through drawers, cabinets, and stacks of papers. She was looking through anything she could find. She was selecting only important-looking documents and stuffing them into a bag.

Kneeling on the floor, Jill spotted a small ball of fur hiding under the couch. "Hey you." She called out reaching her hand towards a small, fluffy cat. "What's your name?" she whispered. The cat walked cautiously up to the bewitching larcenist. "I'll call you Dinah." she said. "Nice to meet you, Dinah." Jill pet the beautiful cat. Little did she know that the cat was already named Ruffles.

Petting the feline was soothing, but Jill knew she had to finish. She took a deep breath and got up, sending the house cat running away from her as fast as he could.

Anna's apartment was now destroyed. Papers had been strewn about, and drawers had been rummaged through and left open. Jill left no corner of the apartment unturned. She didn't want James to have any reason to feel like he needed to come back here.

She even used her phone to take a picture of the mess that she was leaving behind. She sent it to James as proof that he would never have a reason to bother this woman again. *'See, I went through everything!'* the accompanying message said.

It wasn't just a few seconds later when Jill got the warning on her phone from James, telling her the funeral was over.

Anna's apartment had nothing of value worth taking— no cash, no drugs, no fancy jewelry.

Jill did find some medical records; she sorted them and took some, knowing that this would make James happy and keep him quiet.

Jill was content because she knew that she had possibly saved this woman's life from a mentally unstable killer named James.

Jill hurried to finish up. She tucked the rest of the sorted papers into her bag.

As she walked past the small dining room table, her now heavy bag caught a chair, knocking it to the floor in front of her. Jill tripped and tumbled forward. She came to rest on her side, dazed but otherwise unhurt. She collected her belongings, quickly sorting through papers that had flown around when she'd fallen.

Jill picked herself up and swiftly headed home, relieved that it was finally over.

At the same time, in front of the funeral home on the other side of the city, James still sat in the old, rusty, borrowed car and thought about the movie he had just watched. He'd had to intimately meet the man he had killed. It had been way harder than he'd expected any funeral for a dead stranger to be; but then again, this man wasn't a stranger anymore.

Maybe James wasn't as cold as he thought he was.

Chapter 19 – Out West.

James was rumbling along the road in the old borrowed car, driving home from the funeral. He was still thinking about the film. It did make him feel different about the killing.

Unfortunately, his deep thoughts on the topic were suddenly interrupted by a loud wail.

Blue and red lights flashed in James' rearview mirror.

"Fuck…my…life!" he whispered softly.

"Good evening, sir," the officer called out, as he approached the open driver's-side window.

"Good evening, officer," James replied.

"Where are you coming from tonight?" the officer asked.

"Just headed home after a friend's funeral. It was at the funeral home on Western," James said factually.

Luckily, he had a real alibi, he was sober, and he was dressed for the part.

"Well, I noticed you have a brake light out. I just wanted to give you a warning on that," the officer said sternly.

"Can I have your license and registration?" The officer glared at James with a deadly serious face.

"I borrowed the car for the funeral. I don't have a car myself. Here is the registration and my license." The officer returned to his car and ran the data.

James sat in the old, beat-up car, with a missing brake light, and started to sweat.

"Fuck..." he mumbled. What if someone had seen him leaving David's, or what if there was some security footage from the street?

"Fuck...fuck...fuck..." James tapped the steering wheel nervously. Sweat started to roll down his forehead. It beaded on his lips. He tasted the salt. He wiped his forehead dry with his sleeve.

What if he already had a warrant out? James started to panic. He fought back the thought of putting the car in *drive* and fleeing, pedal to the metal, only to ditch the car somewhere and attempt to escape on foot.

James watched in fear as the tall, armed man walked back along the side of the car, stopping at the driver's window. His hand always perched near the handle of his service weapon, holstered on his hip.

"Here you go, James. Tell your friend to get the brake light fixed within thirty days," the cop said, handing the paperwork back with a written warning.

The officer's computer had shown that everything on James came back clear.

"Yes, sir! I'll be sure to," James said with a relieved nod.

"Holy shit!" he said with a laugh as he pulled away. His heart was still pounding. The rush of adrenaline made him feel alive.

James got home about thirty minutes later than Jill. He looked at her as he walked through the front door.

"Okay, we should probably leave town for a while," James said. Now, only after being rattled by the cop, was he finally agreeing with what Jill had been saying all along.

They had stayed long enough for the funeral, and now James wanted to just lie low. They had found documents that they needed to sit down and go through, but they could take those with them. Jill thought part of James' shift toward wanting to leave had to do with him taking his prescriptions. Either way, she wanted to leave too and was happy at the thought of getting away for a short while.

They could be just like Bonnie and Clyde, Jill thought, trying to make a better experience out of all of this. However, up until recently, Bonnie and Clyde had seemed sexy and sadistically romantic.

Now, the idea seemed horrible and the last thing that the stability-seeking woman wanted. Jill truly wanted everything to be positive, so she threw the horrible fantasy of Bonnie and Clyde away. She now just saw the iconic pair as a couple of cold-blooded characters, just like James without his medication.

James told Jill about the police pulling him over. He told the story of the funeral and the film that played.

"Look what I got!" Jill said proudly. She showed James two stacks of reports for different brain testing, mostly pertaining to Bern. They didn't know that these were simply Bern's standard reports from the past two years; Dr. Smith had recently brought them home to review. There was nothing secret about them.

James was happy and this, in turn, made Jill happy. These moments with a normal James were what she lived for.

The couple packed up a few belongings and headed out West in the borrowed, beat-up, 1978 station wagon.

It would be kind of like an adventure; Jill tried to convince herself of this. She remembered family road trips with her brother. They were always fun and full of excitement as they explored new landscapes and passed through random small towns. Her brother had been her best friend growing up.

The couple drove for miles with Jill in the passenger's seat. She held her hand out the open window, feeling the crisp air. Her blonde hair blew in her face like a sexy 1950s pinup girl.

James smiled at her.

The perfect couple rode in a peaceful silence that they hadn't experienced in a long time.

They watched as they passed old cemeteries, crossed stony rivers, and drove through quaint towns.
They were both mostly speechless. It had been so long since either of them had seen anything other than the dirty, crowded city.

It was the beginning of fall, so the air was crisp and cool, especially as dusk fell and their altitude increased as they drove through the snow-peaked mountains.

They drove through several states, some unnecessarily, taking all the scenic routes. They took their time to just enjoy the unplanned trip.

The couple stopped in the mountains for the night. They slept in the station wagon, parked at a pull-off spot along North Fork Highway.

Jill cuddled up next to a stable-minded James, who was now regularly taking his medication. Jill had hidden enough away, that he didn't get a chance to flush them all. Nothing could be more perfect. This was heaven.

The beauty of the spectacular views of the country and the amazing return of her lover had even made Jill forget about David.

She started looking ahead optimistically. Maybe these unfortunate events had been just what they'd needed—a clean start…a new life born out of death. They arrived at Jill's friend's house late the next morning.

"Thanks for letting us stay here," Jill said with sincere appreciation.

"Oh, of course!" he replied with a smile. "Stay as long as you like."

The trio ate lunch, and James listened as the two old friends told stories from years ago.

They laughed at the petty fights they'd had when they'd been young; looking back, the things that had been huge deals to them at that time now seemed ridiculous and laughable.

Jill wondered if, years from now, she would look back at this time in her life and think that everything was petty, ridiculous, and laughable.

Probably not.

After lunch Jill and James went for a walk around the desert oasis where they were staying. They walked hand in hand, as they talked and laughed.

"Hey! Let's go into the city tonight!" James said, with a gleam in his eye.

"You want to?" Jill asked, still surprised by the old James, the man she had grown used to feeling distant from.

"Yeah! Maybe we can gamble a little or get you a new phone. We have our money; we can go spend some of it."

When she'd been packing for this trip, Jill had realized that she had lost her phone. They couldn't find it anywhere, so they had to leave it behind.

The fact that James now called the money he had taken from Jill "their" money, as opposed to *his*, made Jill quickly forgive him for stealing it.

"Can I get a new number too? It would be best to switch numbers after everything that happened. I just want start over completely. "

"Sure. We'll get you a prepaid one. As long as you promise not to lose it this time." James laughed and gave her a nudge.

She looked at him and smiled. She loved *this* James more than anyone ever.

He wasn't craving his usual street drugs; the city was enough of a high. The whole trip had been a high. It was a reality that James didn't want to escape through drugs. Not yet, anyway.

The couple decided to go into Las Vegas and experience the night life of Sin City. It wasn't the ideal vacation spot for freshly stable mental patients and recovering junky strippers, but what the hell...

Later that evening, they called a cab to drive them into the glowing city of sin. They were warmly greeted by the bright, mesmerizing lights.

For a couple of sinners, this place was heaven.

The pair walked down the colorfully lit streets, talking and laughing. They stopped at quirky places and shops—the kind you only find in a city like Las Vegas.

They took pictures of themselves in front of funny wedding chapels, standing next to iconic landmarks, and posing next to goofy signs. The prescriptions had definitely brought the old James back.

The couple stopped for drinks, and they talked and laughed. It was like a real date. Everything clicked again.

Jill had the idea to get a hotel and spend the night in the city to celebrate.

She got the couple of sinners a room at a beautiful hotel. They sat at the bar for one last drink; Jill had a glass of red wine, and James had gin. They watched as gondolas floated along small rivers, creating a romantic atmosphere that was surrealistically foreign.

"Are you ready?" Jill asked, flashing the room key at James.

James nodded with a grin.

The mostly dysfunctional pair walked hand in hand to the luxurious hotel room. Jill got James' prescriptions out of her purse and set them on the bathroom counter. He had been good about taking them since their last fight.

Jill lay on the bed and watched as James took all three pills and washed them down with a handful of water. She slowly removed her clothes, exposing every vulnerability to the man who had proven in the past to be a cold hearted monster and now a cold blooded killer. She lay beautifully naked and exposed. The backdrop was a bright, multicolored, fluorescent, incandescent skyline, as seen through the large windows overlooking the city.

James wiped his mouth and climbed up on the bed with the unguarded, irresistible woman.

Jill slowly climbed on top of him as he lay, on his back on the luxurious bed, with his arms outstretched above his head.

She slowly kissed the side of James' face. The prescriptions had lulled him into an unusually gentle submissiveness that was always welcomed. Jill wasn't afraid of this James—the medicated James. She knew she had to take advantage of the precious time she had though; it was time in heaven that made the rest of her life, which was hell, worth living.

Jill slid along his strong, muscular frame, tickling him with her tongue as she went down.

James laughed at the titillating sensation, and then he gasped loudly.

Jill's mouth felt amazing. She was very playful but also carefully accurate. She made James' leg muscles lock up and stiffen as they stretched underneath the beautiful woman's upper body.

The fluffy pillows surrounded him like the snow angels that Jill remembered making as a little girl. Looking as if he was enveloped in a soft blanket of white in a winter wonderland, his statuesque frame was a radiant sight.

Jill climbed back on top of James and slowly slid him inside of her.

She moaned in a seductive, sexy voice at the feeling of James throbbing deep inside.

She looked down at her lover. He smiled in response to her gaze.

Jill's body slowly slid up and down, her breasts sensually grazing his chest with a light touch.

"I want you on top," Jill commanded the intoxicated, naked man. Her body was now limp and submissive as she fell face-down on the bed. James was definitely starting to feel the drinks that they'd had.

The excited but dazed man smacked Jill's perfectly round ass, leaving a stinging, light-pink handprint. He then climbed on top of her naked body, biting the back of her neck hard enough to leave teeth marks. Jill winced at the mild but pleasurable pain.

James slid inside of her, giving her exactly what she wanted. It made her feel connected and complete. The feeling of sheer ecstasy drove her crazy. She clenched the sheets and bit the pillow, muffling her pleasured screams. Her head stayed buried and face-down as James pushed his body against hers.

James was going to take her higher.

He rolled Jill's luscious body over as she cried out for him not to stop.

Before she could even complete a sentence begging for more, James was already back inside of her soft, wet body.

Jill was on another intoxicating, dopamine-fueled ride into euphoria. James penetrated her more deeply than she could ever remember.

There was no other place Jill would rather be in the world. There was no amount of money that could buy this moment from her.

Jill was in love. She had to be, to tolerate the bad times. It was love that made her tolerant. It was love that made her stay with her lover despite his dark side.

The sound of skin slapping against skin filled the small hotel room and spilled out through the open balcony doors and down to the streets below. A few lucky passersby could hear the pleasurable noises coming from, what sounded like, the heavens above.

James gasped one final time as he finished and pulled himself out of his lover's trembling body.

Jill climbed out from under James as he collapsed with exhaustion and pleasure.

Short of breath and glistening with sweat, she cleaned herself up a little and found a cigarette that she hadn't yet smoked.

She sat naked on the edge of the hotel bed, smoking the cheap cigarette. She blew the smoke towards the open balcony. The soft light shining through the window grazed the delicate curve of her back.

Jill talked to James about how she thought that someday she was going to be a good mom. She talked about how their lives were going to eventually be normal.

She puffed and blew the thick, white smoke out through the open balcony door. The smoke floated away in front of an endless backdrop of brightly lit buildings, only to disappear just a few seconds later.

She talked about their future together. She talked about her love for him.

The open door let the city sounds float in and fill the hotel room with honks, the yells of noisy people, and what sounded like hundreds of feet pounding against the pavement. Even though it was all just noise, it sounded happy.

Jill finished the cigarette and put it out on the balcony railing that overlooked the city of sin below. She looked over at James, who was already sound asleep. He had passed out the minute after he had finished and hadn't even heard a single word she'd said; he wasn't even conscious anymore.

Damn...well, probably for the better, she thought, sadly still in denial about her true loneliness.

Jill turned the light off and, for a change, fell asleep next to her lover. She let her mind fade into darkness.

James moaned and turned away at first; however, Jill's persistence paid off in the long run, and she slept entwined with the one person in the world whom she loved. Jill knew that the medication had brought her James back.

They spent an amazing morning in the desert city. They had breakfast and walked the streets, taking in the sights. They talked about staying and starting over—a new place to start a new, refreshed life together.

"So we were talking about moving out this way," Jill told her friend when they got back to his house.

"Well, please stay as long as you like. If you move, you can always stay here while you get set up," he replied sincerely.

"Thank you." Jill smiled at James and grabbed his hand as he sat next to her.

James and Jill spent almost a week away reconnecting. James had stayed on his prescriptions the whole time and was exactly who Jill wanted him to be.

She fell in love all over again.

The two reluctantly returned to their small home in the dirty city. The ride home was beautiful but somber. They both hated having to return.

The old, loud station wagon rumbled down the highway with its own sad tone.

They drove and talked, enjoying what little time away they had left.

"I really think we should come back here! We could start over again. Things would be better away from the city." Jill thought she would do great working in Vegas.

"No, we should stay in the city," James said, to Jill's surprise.

"But...you agreed earlier?!"

"Yeah, well I changed my mind!" James snapped back.

Jill shut her mouth and stared angrily out the passenger window. She had daydreamed about them moving away from what she felt was a cursed part of the city that they unfortunately lived in. It hurt her to know that James was going to hold them back once again.

The couple drove the rest of the way in near silence. Jill started thinking again about David and the nightmares. She started to remember what her life was really like. What she had left behind was, what she was coming back to. It had been waiting for her.

She remembered what home was really like. Her life away from the city of sin was hell. Sin City, had turned out to be heaven.

The couple got home to the apartment, exhausted and hungry after almost ten hours of driving.

Jill threw a frozen pizza in the oven. The night was mostly silent, other than the sound of the TV.

They watched cartoons and ate pizza. Everything was as good as it could be, given they had returned to their hell.

Chapter 20 – Home Sweet Home.

"I think I'm going to go back to Bern's house and look around myself." James' tone was condescending. He was hinting again that Jill hadn't done a good enough job.

"What?! Why? He doesn't know about any government mind-control project. He's just a painter," Jill defended the innocent man- her gentlemanly one night stand that she couldn't stop thinking about.

"Well, I will see for myself. I'm going to go over there tonight." James was insistent.

"What if he's there? You can't just start breaking into people's houses now!"

"If he is there, maybe I'll shoot him too," James said with a serious laugh.

Jill was now disgusted and scared. She knew that the old James wouldn't hesitate to shoot Bern in cold blood for absolutely nothing.

"Why aren't you taking your medication?" Jill asked, positive that he was on edge because he had stopped taking it at some point. The signs were something that James could never hide.

"I left it back there in Vegas. I'm good though; I don't need it!" James said aggressively, as if he really believed he was okay.

Jill quickly changed the subject to ease the tension.

"Hey, do you know where Kitty has been? I haven't seen him. I put new food out when we left, and it hasn't been touched," Jill said curiously, looking at the untouched bowls in the kitchen.

"Oh, I gave him away to a shelter right before we left," James said emotionlessly. "I thought I told you that. You know I hate cats. I don't even know why I let it stay when I moved in."

"Are you serious? Are you fucking serious?!" Jill exclaimed.

"Yeah, don't worry; he'll probably go to a good home," James said, as he continued to stare blankly at the TV screen.

"That was my fucking cat! Are you fucking serious right now?! You knew how much I loved Kitty! You are such a dick!" Jill's lips quivered, her eyebrows sank, and she started crying as shock and anger turned to sadness.

"He was just a cat! You will get over it in less than a week. You know I don't like cats. That shouldn't be a big deal for you to accept," James said manipulatively.

Jill was done. She wasn't going to argue. In the end, he would still think he was right anyway.

Jill went into their bedroom and locked the door. She flopped over on the bed, trying to be as far away from James as possible.

The distraught woman continued to cry. The vacation was definitely over.

"Let me in, Jill!" he shouted, as he pounded on the door and jiggled the handle.

"No! Go away!" Jill screamed.

James pounded louder and harder. The solid wood door, which was probably as old as the city itself, held strong.

"Jill! Open the fucking door!"

Jill walked to the door and unlocked it out of fear. She knew James would probably ram it with his body or kick it down if she didn't just unlock it. It would be easier this way.

The second that Jill's ears registered the click of the knob unlocking, the door flew open violently.

The edge of the door smashed hard into her cheek, and she heard the sound of her teeth grinding against each other inside her head. Her jaw painfully pushed back from the harsh blow.

The impact stunned her and threw her entire body to the ground. She immediately fell backwards, her hands too slow to catch her fall.

"You don't lock me out of my own fucking bedroom, Jill!" James screamed down at her.

Jill held her face and lay on the ground, still stunned.

James turned and left, grabbing the keys to the old borrowed car from off of the table on his way out.

Jill heard the front door close, followed by the low rumble of the old loaner car as it drove away.

She sat and cried.

She wished this was a nightmare, but it wasn't. Her cat was gone. James really had gotten rid of him, the only friend that was *always* there for her.

Jill hid in bed for the rest of the day, listening vigilantly for James' rumbling return so she could decide to fight or flee—a natural, instinctive decision when an animal is faced with danger.

She was devastated. She knew she could not continue on like this. She was going to have to make some very hard decisions soon.

Unfortunately, being involved in a murder with a mentally ill lover limited her options for a clean breakup.

Jill was suddenly startled by the sound of the front door opening. It was James; she hadn't heard the beat-up, rumbling car because he had returned it to the owner and walked home.

James came through the bedroom door swiftly to find a scared Jill standing next to the wall. She had panicked and wanted to escape but, unfortunately, had nowhere to go.

"Holy shit! I know what we forgot!" James exclaimed.

"What are you talking about?" Jill asked puzzled and scared. She could think of nothing they'd forgotten, especially anything that could be her fault.

"Oh my God! You did it!" James said, with a visible hint of realization written all over his face.

He paced back and forth in front of the doorway. Sweaty and nervous, he was definitely high on something bad—a bad trip...it could be anything.

"You bitch! You fucking moved it! That antique metal box that I set by the door...at David's house. You...fucking...bitch!" James shook his head with an angry glare.

"I don't know what you're talking about!" Jill quickly lied to the irate man.

"You moved it. You made me forget it on purpose! You are a selfish fucking bitch!" James said, as he lunged toward Jill.

"I didn't!" she yelled as she looked, for a split second, at the fury in her lovers eyes.

James mercilessly grabbed Jill by her shoulder-length blonde hair.

"Owwwww! Babe, let go!" she screamed.

He grabbed her wrist and let go of her hair, only so he could grab her other wrist with his free hand. Jill, now completely terrified, stopped fighting back. She knew it would be better to try to calm James down rather than to escalate things.

"Take a deep breath, baby," Jill said calmly. "Please relax. I need you to take your medication. Please don't skip any days. You are too violent without it," Jill said soothingly, still restrained at the wrists by James' strong grip.

"You want me to be something I'm not! You want me to sit there and be a little bitch! You want me to be like you! Well, that's not me! I'm a fucking cold-blooded asshole. That's who I am! You're just too stupid to see it!" James fumed, as his face turned red.

"You are such a dick! I stripped for you, but I'm the selfish one!? Go to hell!" Jill lost control and screamed between sobs.

"What?! You were stripping! You didn't tell me that?! You...FUCKING WHORE!" James grabbed Jill's hair and pulled her toward him.

"Owwwww! I did it for you! For us! I have been through hell for you!" Jill screamed back at the man who had caused her unspeakable pain throughout the years.

"That's why you dyed your hair, you fucking liar! Were you stripping all the other times you dyed your hair blonde!?" Spit flew violently from his mouth, showering Jill's face. James was enraged. He was breathing heavily. The veins in his neck bulged.

"I'm not selfish! I did it to help you! This isn't who you are!" At that precise moment, Jill's heart finally and irreparably broke.

All the hell she had been going through had been because of him. All the hell she had lived every day had been for him. Jill finally acknowledged that James was an ungrateful monster to whom she had given everything; and what she hadn't been able to give him, he had taken. He was never going to change.

"I only did it to get enough money to get your meds, to make you better!" Jill said with a painfully contorted look on her face, as if she felt some of her hair being pulled away from her scalp. She flinched as James raised his clenched fist.

"Fuck you! I bet you fucked that artist guy too! I saw the way you looked at his picture!" he said, brutally throwing her head back against the wall behind her. The room echoed with a dull thud as her skull brutally met the brick.

Jill fell to the floor unconscious. A small amount of blood dripped down the side of her face. All was silent.

In the air hung a horrible feeling of jealous rage and betrayal.

"FUCK!" James screamed. He rubbed his head as he tried to decide what to do now.

He nudged Jill with his foot. She didn't respond; she didn't move.

He dragged her limp body over to the bed and put his devoted lover on the small mattress that they shared.

James grabbed the front of her blouse and ripped it open, sending buttons flying through the air when the strands of thread holding them onto the shirt snapped.

He pulled Jills' pants off—an easy task with no resistance from the unconscious blonde. The jeans were followed by a sexy blue thong, which was the only thing keeping James from what he really wanted.

He threw the skimpy blue lace off to the side where it landed on the night stand, draped over a beloved old copy of *Through the Looking-Glass*.

James slowly spread Jill's legs apart, exposing her beautifully manicured private parts. He put his mouth on the soft, warm skin where her legs met. His tongue teased her lips and made her wet. Even unconscious, she seemed to enjoy being ravaged by James' soft mouth.

James unzipped his jeans and looked down at the luscious, ready, gorgeous stripper body in front of him.

James towered over Jill, who was now dripping wet from his mouth in all the places that mattered the most.

He turned his lover face-down and, pressing his body against hers, he slid easily inside where it was warm and moist. He satisfyingly pushed himself into her as deep as he could go.

James fucked her hard and fast. Her naked body bounced back into his every time he thrust her down into the mattress. Jill didn't make a sound.

James flipped Jill back over like a slutty rag doll. He continued to play with her succulent body without protest.

He climbed on top of her and put his weight between her legs, resting his body on her hips.

Jill awakened to the weight of James on top of her. She was pinned down to the mattress by his solid, muscular frame. His still-clothed body slid between her legs.

"No, James, not like this!" Jill said, half-awake and in a daze. She was confused and wasn't sure what was even happening. Her head was pounding. She was seeing bright spots.

James forcefully penetrated her again. He pushed his way inside of her as she struggled to stop him.

"Ouch...ouch! James, hold on! It hurts! Stop! It hurts! James, PLEASE!" Jill winced in pain and her fearful, hazel eyes started to water.

She tried to move but couldn't. James' strength dominated her. Jill tried to adjust her body to make the pain less intense, but James wouldn't let her.

He grabbed her hands and held them down, above her head. Jill struggled to break free.

"Stoooooopppppp!" she screamed at the top of her lungs.

James immediately covered Jill's mouth with his large, heavy hand, muffling any sound from the tense, unwilling yet submissive woman.

His naked body violently slammed against hers. The sound of skin slapping violently against skin filled their small apartment.

James' strong arms easily flipped Jill back over onto her stomach; she had no chance of stopping him. James grabbed Jill's arms and pinned them behind her back at the wrists. He held her wrists together with one hand and kept them just above her lower back.

From behind, he put his other hand over her mouth, muffling any of her additional attempts to cry out.

The pillow was now wet with a dark maroon stain where the blood continued to slowly drip from the back of Jill's head.

Jill's thighs shook as James pounded his body into hers. The pressure of his body crushed her small frame. The feeling was undeniably erotic for her, even under the horrific circumstances.

She tried to scream but couldn't. She was terrified. She didn't want to have an orgasm, but James' stiff rod excited her, even through the pain and discomfort.

James thrust against Jill's naked backside one final time.

James finally let go of her mouth and wrists as his body and mind relaxed.

Jill was throbbing. "Stop! It hurts!" she cried out again.

He slid out from inside of her.

"Why didn't you stop?!" Jill screamed, her face covered in tears and smeared blood.

"Come on! You know you liked it!"

"Fuck you! It fucking hurt! You are such an asshole! I hate you!" she screamed.

James angrily grabbed Jill's throat with both hands, startling her. The pressure of his thumbs made Jill gag and want to cough. Very little air was getting through past the abusive man's hands, and it was quickly becoming less and less until she could no longer breathe at all.

Jill clawed James' arms as she tried to break free from his grip. She was panicking, and her brain was running out of oxygen. Things became fuzzy. She started turning purple. Then...silence.

James let go of Jill's throat; her face was now blue with a light hint of purple.

Her body was, once again, limp and lifeless.

James grabbed the belt from Jill's pants, that he had forcefully removed, and wrapped it around her legs, making it as tight as possible. He rolled her limp body over and wrapped an extension cord, that he pulled out of the wall, around her wrists, tying her hands together behind her back.

Next, James shakily fumbled through all of the junk in the apartment until he found an old, almost gone, roll of duct tape. He ripped a piece off with his teeth and put the short strip of the heavy, grey tape across Jill's delicate mouth.

"Damn it!" he said, as he began to panic.

Jill's beautiful face was smeared with the blood that still trickled from her gouged scalp. Mixing with sweat.

"FUCK!" James yelled, as he started to pace faster.

Reality quickly set in. Murder could be such a buzzkill.

He needed to clear his mind; he needed fresh air. He grabbed his apartment keys and walked outside.

James walked around the city for a few hours, contemplating what to do next. He sat on a bench in the park. He walked along dark alleys. He was trying to find an escape for his mind.

He stopped and stared at himself for a while in a dark store window. The reflection he saw was someone he didn't even recognize anymore. He *had* become a monster.

James walked a few more miles to go see a guy who could get him high. He needed to calm down. He knew it would be okay if he could just get a fix and then go back and deal with what happened.

He met his friend, and they snorted some coke together and talked. Once James felt calm, he headed home. The cocaine had helped the reality of the situation melt away as if nothing had happened.

As he came back around the corner of the block, returning home from his long walk, he saw a police car in front of his apartment building. Its blue and red lights flashed against the bricks, illuminating everything around. James turned around and casually walked the opposite direction.

The police were only briefly stopped out front after pulling a car over for having a headlight out, however, the nervous murderer still didn't want to take any chances.

Jill woke up, gasping for air but quickly realized that she could only breathe through her nose. She found that she couldn't move her arms or legs. She was dazed and confused.

What the hell happened? she thought.

Jill managed to sit herself up, leaning her back against the headboard. Her head was pounding; the pain was intense. She could see dried blood on the floor where she had first fallen by the wall. There was a smeared trail that led over to the bed; it was the path along which James had dragged her, like a line drawn crudely in red ink.

She quickly realized that she was tied up. She now started to remember the argument and James pulling her hair. The sound of her skull grinding against the dirty, brick wall was one of the last things that she could remember.

After a few minutes, she managed to get her hands free of the extension cord and the belt off her ankles.

She pulled the duct tape off of her mouth. It hurt like hell as it ripped away, leaving the skin underneath raw and her lips sore.

Jill realized that she was naked, wet, and freshly fucked. This triggered the memory of waking for a few minutes with James on top of her, his hand on her mouth. Jill grabbed her sore neck as the memories became clearer. She remembered how it felt to almost die.

Jill was afraid to call the police because of David's murder and the break-ins. If they came and linked James to anything, she was sure that he would take her down with him.

Bruised, battered, and bloody, she lay in bed for a few minutes and cried. She went to the bathroom and cleaned herself up. The gouge in her head stung as the hydrogen peroxide foamed on the wound. Jill closed her eyes tightly, waiting for the pain to disappear. She held a washcloth against her head until the pain was finally under control.

She looked at her fingernails, noticing that one was now broken. She looked closely and found that three others had skin tucked underneath them—skin that had been ripped from her abusive lover as she'd tried to claw her way free, in attempt to get a breath of air.

Jill finished cleaning herself up and contemplated what to do now. She wanted desperately to run away. She wanted to head back out west alone, but she knew that

James would come looking for her, starting in Las Vegas, assuming that is where she would go. Unfortunately, she had no other place to go to, no other escape. She had no other options.

Jill's heart sank instantly as she once again heard the unmistakable sound of the front door opening...

Chapter 21 – The End is the Beginning.

Jill gasped silently as she tried to hold herself together. She needed to try to be strong.

She watched the attractive, strung-out man walk through the front door as if nothing had happened. Jill knew that she had to take control.

"Hey." He said.

"I really wish you would take your medication," she said. Her mood was now solemn and forced, her voice monotonous and hollow.

James seemed only half-stunned to see her free. He was obviously very high on something now.

"Well, that ain't me, baby," James said, as he brushed his golden- blonde hair back with his hand. He blew Jill a superficial kiss.

Jill handed James two pills and said, "I got these for you before we left. If you aren't going to take your prescriptions then you at least need to get high more often."

She knew James wouldn't have a problem taking street drugs, or anything else, as long as it wasn't his prescriptions.

James took the pills and swallowed them with a mouthful of water from the sink. He then lay down on the couch.

"Thanks," he said, looking as if he had spent the day fighting demons, both mentally and physically.

"No problem. I just want you to be happy. I don't want to make you be someone you aren't," Jill spoke vacantly.

She looked at her face in the mirror. Her lip was swollen now, and her cheek had started to show some purple bruising. Luckily, it was faint enough to be hidden with some light makeup.

*Time heals all...*she thought. It's what her mother had always told her.

The morphine Alice had given to James had been twice the normal dose that he usually took. She knew he would sleep well tonight.

"What do you think about God?" Alice asked James.

"What?...I don't," James said in a puzzled tone, as his voice trailed off. He was dead asleep within minutes.

Jill sat and watched the mystery-solving cartoon gang on TV. The gang solved the riddle with the help of their canine companion. Of course, it was Old Man Jenkins in the ghoul costume again. It usually was.

James' heavy head now lay in Jill's lap. She brushed the blonde hair out of his face as she stared warmly at the man she still loved.

"Maybe I'm just like you," Jill said, holding James' head in her hands. His muscles were relaxed, and his head moved feely. A part of Jill wanted to just snap his fucking neck right then and end everything, but she didn't think that was a good idea. She couldn't do something like that, even if he deserved it. She gently slid her body out from under his and let his head rest back down onto the couch.

Alice walked to the bathroom and removed a syringe and a box of bandages from the medicine cabinet.

She opened the box of bandages and pulled out a small bag of heroin that she had purchased from the strip club manager earlier in the week.

"Hello, old friend," Alice said, looking at the white chunks. "I need you now more than ever before."

She put the drug in a spoon and held a lighter under it, waiting for it to liquefy and boil, just as she had done for so many years as a junky. During that period in her life, moments like these had been all she'd lived for.

Heroine had been her escape—a lifestyle to which she never wanted to return.

She sucked the liquid smack into the syringe through the opening in its sharp needle. This would be her escape once again—a way to get away from everything.

"This should be plenty," she said softly, as she flicked the syringe, letting any air bubbles escape.

Alice was truly ready for this. This was something she had wanted for a long time.

She took a belt and wrapped it around James' arm, making the veins in it bulge.

Alice always did the dirty work.

She quickly stuck the needle directly into the biggest vein that she saw. She slowly depressed the plunger as she watched the liquid deliberately empty out. She then let go of the belt. He didn't even flinch.

"We really tried. We will never forgive you for everything. You know that you deserved to be punished," Alice said spitefully. She personally, had never liked James.

"I love you and always will," Jill said to the unconscious lover lying next to her on the couch. She brushed James' hair out of his face one last time. "No regrets..." she whispered with tears in her tired, hazel eyes.

Jill stood up and stared down at James. She had loved that man. She had tried to make it work. It was time to let go.

"Maybe I am just like you..." she said once more, as she looked at the needle still piercing his vein. A small trickle of blood had started to flow from the tiny hole where the stainless steel had punctured his skin.

James' body gently twitched and convulsed. His breathing became slow and shallow.

From inside James' poisoned body, his lungs struggled to take one last breath, his eyes fluttered behind his eyelids, and then...nothing. James' body lay still on his couch. Overdosed.

Everything seemed so tranquil. Time slowed to a crawl. Jill didn't hear a single sound. Deep down inside, she knew it was good for James to finally let go.

She was very sad for the incredible loss, but, at that moment, Jill experienced a sense of stillness that she had never felt before. Death wasn't like in the movies. It wasn't scary or dreadful; it was the most peaceful time she had ever experienced in her entire life. She was free. He could never hurt her again. The abuse was finally over.

"Goodbye, James," Jill said, as she kissed him on the forehead.

Slowly, with tears streaming down her face, she walked around their small one-bedroom apartment.

Jill had already packed up most of what she owned earlier in the week. She'd thrown away whatever she didn't want, and James hadn't noticed. She knew that he wouldn't.

Jill somberly walked around to each of the small rooms. She packed up anything else that tied her to James, which, for all the years they had spent together, wasn't that much—one or two pictures and a couple of personal items.

Jill copied the pictures from Las Vegas on James phone and saved them to hers. All the memories of the good times with the man she loved…not the monster he really was. She laughed and cried as she looked at them together in the photos. She wished that the week away could have become their life; she hadn't known at the time that those would be their last happy memories together.

Was she really using the prescriptions to force him to be somebody he wasn't? Had she really become that person? Jill wondered. She knew that she would probably never really know.

She erased everything from James phone, then threw it on the ground and stomped on it. The screen shattered and plastic pieces flew.

She finished up and dried her tender, hazel eyes. It was time to get going. She got out the bottle of brown hair dye and washed away Alice's blonde hair with the dusky brown that was Jill. She dyed her hair in the sink, rinsed off in the shower, and then got dressed.

One last look at James; he looked content. Jill knew that he was at peace not having to fight his demons any longer—a tormented, failing mind that was finally at rest.

She whispered "Goodbye, James," and slowly, with tears streaming down her face, left their tiny downtown apartment for what would be the last time.

As she calmly walked to the train station, she considered what she had done. She relived the rage that made her want to snap James' neck. *Was Alice's forced overdose satisfying enough? Yes. It was. He didn't deserve to suffer, but he didn't deserve to live,* Jill thought to herself.

As she crossed the Fourth Street bridge on foot, she stared at the water churning below. It was both beautiful and turbulent, just like her life.

She had taken her large sum of stolen money back from James, and with it, Jill made her first stop at the familiar pharmacy.

"I need to fill a prescription."

"Name?" the pharmacist asked.

"Jill Day," the polite, sexy brunette answered with a smile.

"Okay. It looks like it hasn't been filled for quite a few months. I am going to need the doctor to renew the prescription. They should have nurses on call that can fax it over. I'll give them a call now," the woman in the white coat said.

"Ok, thank you. I'll just wait," Jill replied.

She sat and read a magazine for about fifteen minutes, then the pharmacy tech got her attention.

"They just faxed it over. It will be just a few minutes before it's filled."

"Can I get as many months in advance as I'm allowed, please? I'm going out of state for a few months and figure it would just be easier," Jill said. But, in reality she just wanted to stay untraceable where she was going.

"Sure, the prescription will let me give you six months. Without insurance that will be...$673.21."

She paid for her prescriptions with the money that Alice had stolen from Bern. Jill left the drugstore with the drugs she needed to treat her own dissociative identity disorder. Formerly known in the scientific community as, multiple personality disorder.

At a young age, the condition had been attributed to abuse from her frightening and unpredictable father.

Early on, Jill started associating herself with the character from her favorite book. Alice was a personality that Jill used to escape her father's abuse and her mother's heart-wrenching sadness and hopelessness. Alice's personality became an innocent way to retreat and cope with the reality of the young Jill's turbulent life, at a time when reading the book alone started to fail as an escape.

When Jill was originally diagnosed with what, at the time, was called multiple personality disorder, the doctors had discovered a few other personalities or 'alters'. These characters mostly stayed subdued and rarely surfaced.

Jill related to Alice because of the association with her favorite book, her favorite story, the only thing she had left from her mother. In her late teenage years, Alice quickly became a more dominant and almost only other personality.

After her brother's premature death, followed years later by her depressed mother's suicide, Alice became a more calculating, devious, malevolent personality who became capable of things that Jill was not. Jill knew how to use Alice when she needed to. Jill had learned, for the most part, how to control Alice.

She hadn't been taking her prescriptions lately because of the cost. She had been focused on trying to buy James his. But now, she was going to be back on the antipsychotic drugs for the next six months at least.

She was going to take care of herself, instead of an undeserving lover, for a change.

This meant that the sinister Alice would be going away and staying away. Jill wouldn't be able to rely on her any longer.

She took the first dose of her prescription with a bottle of water that she bought at the pharmacy.

This was Jill officially starting over...completely alone. Without James. Without Alice.

She got on a train and headed back out west to stay with her friend once more. She was going to start her life over.

She thought about James and her father and how, if it hadn't been for her father's mistreatment, she probably wouldn't have put up with James for as long as she had. A vicious cycle of cruel abuse had now finally been broken, thanks to Alice.

Jill watched the world pass by as the train slid swiftly along the tracks. The wheels clicked and clacked as they rolled forward toward a whole new life.

Jill knew she would probably never come back to this city—the city where James had died.

The good thing about dead junkies, like James, was that the cops didn't look very hard for a reason why they overdosed. Case closed.

And with that thought Jill realized that she was now, at last, truly free. She was free from James. She was going to be free from Alice.

She left the conspiracy theories and the search for answers about nefarious government plans behind her. As far as she was concerned, they had died with James.

She sat on the train, her body slowly swayed with the tracks. She watched out the window with a smile, as the world passed by in a blur of color. It felt like a new world now. Bright and vibrant.

Starting over in Las Vegas alone, she knew that she was going to be just fine.

She could tell...this was the beginning of something big.

Vinal Lang

****

"Life is neither good or evil, but only a place for

good and evil."

~Marcus Aurelius

****

The End is the Beginning…

****

…a word from the author.

I hope you enjoyed this story. I know it was gritty and in your face but the story of what caused the events of book one, Keeping Minds, needed to be told. I hope you enjoyed the intimate relationship between the two and found it a unique reading experience.

Hopefully, this story made you rethink book one, Keeping Minds. You can now look back and see all the little details that you missed; things you may not have questioned the significance of.

I tied in items from the literary classics *Alice in Wonderland* and of course *Through the Looking Glass*, both by Lewis Carroll. I hope you found and enjoyed some subtle references and quotes.

I wrote the first two books alongside each other so that I could keep the stories very close, yet make sure they are each their own, complete story, with their own characters. I tried to really weave the two stories as much as possible without you realizing it or letting those things become distractions.

As with the first book, I hope you felt a range of emotions ranging from shock, awe, sadness, love, joy, pain and lust...to name a few.

I also hope you enjoyed the change of perspective and maybe even experienced something new.

The next book, Losing Minds will continue where these two both ended. It is definitely the most intricate of the stories so far, with the most surprises and twists. Of course, we will go back and pick up, with Bern and Anna, where we left off. It should be a very fun and unforgettable ride.

Thanks for reading.

~Vinal Lang

Vinal Lang

* * * * * **PLEASE READ!** * * * * *

As the author of *Failing Minds*, this page is, in my view, the most important of them all

If you find yourself or a loved one in an abusive relationship, please do not take the path of the character Jill, tolerating the abuse, or Alice, engaging in dangerously destructive retaliation. There are many organizations that can provide help and assistance for free. I have compiled the following short list of places to start if you do need help:

The National Domestic Violence Hotline
www.thehotline.org
1-800-799-7233

HopeLine
www.hopeline.com
1-800-442-4673

National Center on Domestic and Sexual Violence
www.ncdsv.org

BadBitchesHaveBadDaysToo.com

There are also many places that can help with drug abuse. I am sure that any of the organizations above could put you in contact with the right people if they cannot help themselves.

Thank you for reading. Much love. ☺ ~ Vinal

Made in the USA
Columbia, SC
15 November 2022